WildFire • **Janet Paisley**

Taranis Books

design by Alan Mason

ISBN 1 873899 50 5

Taranis Books acknowledges the assistance of the Scottish Arts Council in the publication of this volume.

Printed by Clydeside Press, High Street, Glasgow
Published by Taranis Books,
2 Hugh Miller Place, Edinburgh EH3 5JG

Photo: Campbell H. Morrison

Janet Paisley grew up in the village of Avonbridge and was educated at Falkirk High School and Callander Park College of Education. She has lived in Essex, Devon and several Central Scotland villages. Her varied occupations have included bus conductress, waitress, shop assistant, market trader, laboratory assistant and primary teacher in Livingston Station and Harthill. A divorced single parent, she now lives in Glen Village with her six surviving sons.

Janet is well-known as a poet, appearing regularly at most major Scottish festivals. Her poetry collections include **Pegasus in Flight** and **Biting Through Skins** (both published by Rookbook) and the video **Images** (Moray House). Her work for children has been used in schools and on radio and television. A frequent guest in schools and writers groups, Janet was writing fellow for Glasgow South Divisiion Libraries 1990-92. **Wild Fire** is her first collection of stories.

ACKNOWLEDGEMENTS
LONG HAUL was originally published in Behind the Lines,Third Eye Centre 1989. SOOANS NICHT appeared in the anthology New Writing Scotland 8 (1990) and DUE in New Writing Scotland 9 (1991) both published by the ASLS. WIDDERSHINS was included in Original Prints4 published by Polygon (1992). STEPPIN OOT was in Scottish Short Stories 1992, published by Harper Collins. HOMECOMING appeared in Parcel of Rogues, Clocktower Press (1992). HOMECOMING was first published in Spectrum in February 1992. LAST INJUN appeared in Northwords in 1993.

For my sons
Michael, Christopher, Jonathan, Mark, Laurence, David,
Matthew.

> .... *I hold you here*
> *against distortion; knowing that love*
> *is work, is hard we know as breaking stones,*
> *and desperate distance even when*
> *the breath comes close.*

(Inchcolm - Alexander Hutchison)

THE PROMPTER

She didn't live with me. That you must understand first of all. And I can't say we were close, though many times I wished that to be true. She was always around though. Even in childhood. Then, her eyes were full of dreams and she didn't see the smallness of the streets we were both chained to. Took no account of them. She refused to acknowledge the possibility of an unsevered umbilical cord. Four walls couldn't contain her. Nor a few hundred houses.

"Bricks," she would say. "They're only bricks."

I met her, the first time, on top of a cliff. She was standing there, looking at the sky with her head tilted back and breeze lifting her hair. I scrambled up red rock onto the springy grass. She didn't move, just stood there, gazing up at the clouds while gingham flapped round her knees and her hair moved. I looked down at the village, tidy and organised from this height. Red roofs, black slate, pebble dash and stone.

"It looks small," I said.

"It is small. Look." She put out her arm, pointed a finger and touched the top of the church spire way across on the opposite side of the valley. I was game. In the streets, I spotted Isa Cameron, recognisable by her wrap-around pinny and her audience. Squinting down my own arm, I fastened thumb and index finger on her shoulders.

"I could do it. I could pick her up. Put her on top of the church spire."

"Retribution?" she questioned.

"Sharp, anyway. Like her tongue. For her sins."

"No such thing," she said. "Look at him." She was still staring at the sky. It was massive, blue, white, indigo, moving and changing. A black speck hung against cobalt, pinned there by song. She pointed, put her forefinger on the speck.

"If you don't come down," she said. "I'll squash you." The lark dropped like a stone. I was five years old.

After that, I was constantly aware of her presence. In school, where she sat dreaming, I struggled, sweating and stammering, to remember that four sevens were twenty eight. Grotesquely aware of my own inabilities, I'd catch sight of her drifting through lessons as if she knew it all and anyway it wouldn't matter in the end. She was always eloquent. A grasshopper, indifferent to the elements.

"What do teachers know of rain," she'd say. "In twenty eight days the moon waxes and wanes. Time isn't marked on a clock."

Storms excited her. I saw her once, in my back garden, face upturned watching lightning split the night sky. I could tell from the way her head rolled as the thunder growled that she was ecstatic. Everyone else was in bed and she, out of doors in the belting rain, conducted the storm. That was the first time she seemed frightening to me. I let the curtain drop and slid back under the blankets before she caught sight of my white face staring at her through wet glass.

Sometimes she would pass me things. A black pebble, a bleached bone. They were put in my hands as if they were treasure. I could never explain them.

"What are you playing with? Give it here." The imperative Miss Davis. Cheeks burning with mortification, I'd pass the object over and bow my head to the inevitable humiliation, the scathing mockery that would follow. "Full of beasts. Filthy child," and "Have you nothing better to amuse you?" A blue-black feather was consigned to the bin where it would taunt me all day long, begging the impossible rescue.

She never played. Among the other children I was safe from her strange interventions. Yet, when I was alone, wandering the fields or the small woods, and she came up to me, I was always glad of her company. Mesmerised by her differentness.

"See. They are born, mate, die. They eat and are eaten. Functional, they are, cogs that keep the great wheel turning." We were lying on our bellies on the grass ledge above the quarry, watching young rabbits down in the scrub below.

"Don't they have souls, then?" I asked. She looked at me and her eyes were burning.

"Do people? Watch out for the traps. Cogs relate only to other cogs. What can a bird do that you can't?"

"I can sing."

"They're not put in cages because they sing," she said. I stood up and looked back down at the village. People moved about the streets, ant-like, being born, mating, dying. I ran away from her that day. Back into the big round blood-fullness of folk. I wanted them to have souls then. It tormented me for years.

I didn't see her for some time. Had grown up, married, borne children. Then she was back in my life, tantalising from the edges as I worked through separation and divorce. But she was different, often bitter.

"Have you had enough of the wheel? Aren't you broken yet?" I often wondered if she despised resilience.

Sometimes she tormented me about my sexuality. In the livingroom, one warm afternoon when, outside, the sunlight hugged trees, grass, road as if it was permanent and people had to push through the lightness of it, she made me look at reality.

"See," she said, turning my head towards the window.

Outside, two of my neighbours walked by, two men walking greyhounds, oblivious to everything except their own engrossing maleness. "Look," she said. And they were blood and flesh, nail-paring, teeth-baring, hair sprouting, snouted, rutting animals, unnaturally upright and ridiculously evil. The smell of semen and sour sweat clung to them. I was immobilized with the horror of it. They masqueraded in clothes! A sense of alarm, differentness and despair engulfed me. How had I come to this place? My alienation was sudden and complete.

We spent a lot of time together then. Almost but never quite lovers, she taunted me with the openness of her mouth, the fullness of her breasts, the rich swell of belly and thigh. When she kissed me, tongues touching, I believed it was all possible, the belonging in time, space, person. Maybe I chose to ignore it when her teeth caught my lip, drawing blood.

"Fusion is only possible through passion," she said. "I don't mind when you have men. Viewfinders need to be focused. But fire, even in the forest, can only be temporary. Fuel runs out and what are you left with?"

We ran into trouble over the ashes. There were just so many urns could sit comfortably side-by-side on my mantelpiece. When I told her this she raged at me.

"Love! Is it love that looks in a mirror for reflection? Is it love that wants comfort, safety, discretion? Now ... now, after all, you'll put fear up for worship. Call it by name, then. Tell me you want out. Tell me you've met up with the coward in you. But don't tell me love." She wouldn't allow degrees, definitions were reductive, minimalist.

The truth is I wanted in. At least in a cage food and water arrive at regular intervals. I was tired. The umbilical cord, uncut, still shining wet, stretched back a long way. Even if it was only to be temporary, I needed rest.

She stopped coming to me when I stopped living as I

believed. Hasn't been around for some years. The women in the village talk to me now. Two of them were at my door tonight with a petition. We're all on the same side, aren't we. For the first time, I feel myself ageing. My bones disintegrate audibly and every morning the shadows are deeper in the lines on my face. Now I slide into bed long before our used-to-be witching hour. Sometimes, just as sleep takes my last thought away, I can hear her mocking laugh.

SOOANS NICHT

"Ye'll be waantin yer tea."
Iain sut doon, didnae luk it hur. He wis bent ower, takin his bitts aff.
"Aye."
"Ye'll be waantin ower by efter."
This time he lukt it me, fur a meenut, bit he stull sayd it.
"Aye."
His mither snoartit. That wis aw richt then. Fur hur that wis aw richt then. She'd telt him whit wis whit an there wis an end o it. Ah nivir enturd hur heid. Iain pued aff the ither bitt an sut baith doon bi the hearth. He kep his heid bent an widnae luk it me whin ah pit his soup oan the table. Ah couldnae huv lukt back neithur. No noo. No noo it wis aw areenged.
Bit that didnae stoap me flinchin whin ma skirt brushed his chair. Nur ma airm fae touchin his shouder is ah went by the back o him. Ah sweer ah wis nivir that close. Yit he nivir moved. An ah hud meant tae gie him a wide berth. Funny hoo they things dinnae stoap happenin even whin ye dinnae mean thum.
Nane o us spoke while we ett. She wisnae bothert. She nivir

thocht. It wis aw sortit, wisn't it. Nae mair sortit than a chippit egg. He wis burnin me fae the ither side o the table. He wis keepin his heid doon an no lettin oan an he wis hoat up agin me an naewhaur near me an by the time he goat up an went ben the scullery ah could nae mair stoap masell than flee in the air.

Ah stood up slaw enough. Ah cleart the table. Ah walked ben the scullery like it wis easy, naturul. She nivir even lukt it ma back. She'd sortit it. That's aw.

He wis sut oan the stool. Pittin oan his guid shune. Aye, bit he watched me like. Ah pit the dishes in the sink. Ah lukt it him. Ah nivir moved, ah sweer it. He nivir moved. We wur jist thegither. Kissin an touchin an haudin. Like we'd nivir git thegither. Ur be thegither. Like it couldnae be done. Like we wur tryin tae git intae the wan skin an couldnae make it. Ah dinnae ken wha stoapt, him ur me. Ah dinnae ken hoo he goat back oan the stool, nur me it the sink wi the watter rinnin. Bit ah'm shakin an cauld, an steady fur aw that. Ah luks it him.

"Ye're gaun ower by?"

"Aye." He says. "Ah'm gaun ower by."

Ah wantit tae say "Whey? Whey ur ye daen this?" Bit ah kent whey. Ah wantit tae say "She's no fur you, she's a cauld stick an she'll bring ye nuthin an ye'll nivir be fu an gled an warum in yer bed till ye're deid." Ah wantit tae say a million an wan things an there wis nae pint. Nae pint at aw fur he wis gaun ower by an that wis an end o it.

He stuid up an stampt his feet. He pit his haun oan the door knob. Ah hud the plate in ma fingurs. Weel, it jist taen ower. Ah jist flung it doon. Hard like. It ma feet. An luftit anither. An anither, an anither. Ah ken ah wis makin a noise, like greetin bit it wis mair screamin. Iain wis froze it the door, his een jist wide, jist fixt oan me. Couldnae move bit ah wisnae takin that in. Wis his mither goat a haud o me. Hur big heavy airms roon me. Peenin me doon, keepin me stull, haudin me, haudin me.

"Lassie, lassie whit's wrang wi ye. Luk whit ye're daen. Whit's up?" An hur airms ur like irn baurs roon mine. No hurtin, jist haudin me fae the shakin an the noise that wis stoapin noo an Iain wis stull staunin, haun oan the door knob, white in his face an jist lukin. Like a photie fae the auld yin's drawer.

"Come oan ma hen, come oan ma hen," she's gurglin it me, puen ma heid oan hur shouder, stull haudin me. Jist is weel. Ah kin stull hear hur fae this moarnin. *Ye kin go the nicht. Dae yer courtin in the wintur. Ye'll be ower busy come spring.* So he's goatae go the nicht.

Ma face is wet. Hur hair's gittin wet. Smells o mulk, like the scullery. Like the coos. Aw ah kin see is hur ear, an yin fat roon rid lobe. Ah'll mind that ear. Ah'll mind that ear whin ah'd deid, an ah ken it.

"Jenny." He's moved. He's sayd ma name.

She snoarts it him.

"Awa wi ye. Ah'll soart it."

An he goes.

SINGING IN THE DARK

She was going up the road and singing. *I have happiness in my soul* - the words of the song bubbled out of her. Sometimes loud to the trees and sometimes, when someone passed by going down to the village, she kept the sound of it, singing on, inside her head. But there weren't many people. It was afternoon and most folk were at work so she had the peace of an empty road to sing along. It was good to be out of the house, to be away from the oppressiveness of family and being bound by the past in the present. But she wasn't thinking about that, just about the day with its warm sun low in the sky for it was spring and afternoon, and her singing.

Over the brig, she turned at the fork in the road, heading for Armadale. It was a three mile walk but not far on a good day. And this was her birthday. Seventeen she was and free. She smiled at the thought, putting her head back and her shoulders straight. It had taken forever to get to be seventeen and she wasn't going to think about that forever, not today. Just about being there, at last, and walking the road to Armadale, and singing.

The road would be shorter now she wasn't a child though she'd never complained. That was because she walked it going somewhere, even when she was young. Then it had been to visit her aunt and uncle. Their sweet shop had been a treasure trove full of glowing colour and fizzing tastes. Every child's dream. Now it was Tom and the salt-sweetness of his skin and the warm blood-smell in the curve of his neck and her craving for him that could never be satisfied and was satisfying because it filled her, and was real, and was hers. She smiled again and the song burst out of her startling a sheep that was outside the fence so that it jumped to get back in the field and snagged itself, leaping frantically till its strength forced it through.

They would say it was her voice frightened the sheep, that she couldn't sing. But today she didn't care. Today she was going to meet Tom and something new was rising inside her, something expansive. As if she were opening out. As if the day she walked in could become the world she lived in. Today she could sing. Out in the open air where no-one could hear, she could sing all she wanted. The sheep would have jumped anyway, at anyone passing, and the birds didn't mind. It was afternoon and they were fairly quiet, being busy sitting or fetching, but she could hear a lark high above, and another further away. Peewits called to each other and a yellow-hammer flew out of the hedge, dipping low along the verge to draw her away from a nest she'd no interest in anyhow.

"Save your energy," she laughed and went on singing.

She was coming up for the woods, where trees skirted the road on either side, shutting off the open fields. Rooks cawed in the branches, pigeons fluttered and purred, sometimes flopping above the road to the trees opposite. She was into the dark tunnel a way when she realised the song had gone. It had been with her all day, an echo that kept bubbling up, repeating on her. Now it was gone, the sunlight cut off from the road by the trees and her watching the darkness between them and the narrow gap of road ahead.

"Stop this," she told herself. But there was no stopping it. She didn't like this part of the road, the darkness, the shut-inness, the secretive way it had of closing out the day. She glanced back at the sharp triangle of bright fields and sunlit sheep. So easily had she walked out of that into this dark tunnel, thinking the day would come with her, and that the song would stay in her mouth. A memory of home jumped to the front of her mind. Him in his chair, reaching for her, with that strangeness about him. And the child her, transfixed, not knowing the way out. She walked quicker, hearing her feet.

She would sing. How did it go again? Stop watching the trees. She liked trees. But not the shadows between them. Not the silences trapped by these dark, branchless trunks. No, it wasn't even that. It was this place. Deep in the trees was a house. A house that couldn't be seen from the road, nor from any of the fields around as far as she knew. It was a shut-in house and she had no idea if anyone still lived there. And if they did, who they were.

A feeling like bird wings beat in her chest as she passed the stone gateway. Walking fast, she came up to where the road forked. Turn right, she heard herself think. But that would take her off the road, away from Armadale, away from Tom. Her fingers touched the silver chain at her throat. His present, a St. Christopher. She walked on. Two hundred yards of trees met and touched above the road, two hundred yards of dark tunnel, broken wall, damp road and weeds and there, the bright wedge of sun and green that said she'd be back in the daylight soon.

How did it go? The flutter of bird wings in her chest beat again. A blackbird, sickeningly warm and heavy. Something awful was near her. Don't think it, she thought. When she was young the bad things had followed the warning thought as surely as she'd realised it. But she wasn't young now. She was seventeen, outside where it was safe, and could think as she pleased. The triangle of day was brighter, bigger, closer.

Then a shadow moved from the shadows. A shape stepped between her and the light. The blackbird in her chest leapt into her throat. The shape was a man who looked around, behind, at the bright empty road then at her, faltering now, still in the dark and having lost the way out of it.

DUE

It's early moarnin an the mist's risin aff the gress, hingin ablow the trees like a curtin fae thur branches. It suits me. Ah'm no in masell. A coo lous wi burth pain faur doon the holla. A wey aff fae cauvin bit kennin it. Ma feet ur sodden yit there's nae mindin in me. Mibbe the haar is passin through me tae.

Only the shoatgun is soalid. Heaviur, greyur, cauldur. Soalid, richt enough. It cairryin me. Cairryin me doon the field, ower the burn's ruckled stanes, through its white watter an up by the mill.

There's nae a sowl aboot an ah luk back tae see a licht come oan in yin hoose. Rab Coannell gittin up fur the post. Ah keep ahint the mill, doon tae the coattages. The weeds ur high here an thur wetness wid tie thum roon me. Ye jist keep shovin.

Ootside his hoose there's nae back gairden. Jist the wildness an the wet. Close tae the stanes huv the braith o the wurld oan thum. A licht goes oan it ma shouder, dull yella. Watter rins, tinny, intae a kettle. There is whustlin. Saft, nae tune, mind elsewhaur whustlin.

Ah dinnae waant these meenuts o his day. The waashin. The tea made, drunk. Ah waant the slammin o his door. Feet oan his graivel path. The key in his gairidge padloak. Ah waant the luk oan his face is he turns roon.

THE CHERRY TREE

It's an ordinary cherry tree, I tell myself. It was an ordinary kiss. But I know that's not true. About either.

The cherry tree stands at the bottom of our garden. It has stood there for more years than anyone can remember. Which is all Mother has ever said about the tree. I believe she never really sees it. I wonder if she saw that kiss. If her silence meant she understood. Or maybe she never saw me either.

I used to hide in the cherry tree when I needed to be out of the way. Summer was best. It was bushiest then, dense and sheltering. Then, in autumn, the branches litter with red. The stony earth where she stands is strewn with bare, picked clean-and-white pips. After the fruit the leaves just go. No drama. She appears one day stark and bare. Snow and ice are all that make her beautiful then. Crisp mornings, when even the chickens' breath smokes as they scratch about the yard, the cherry tree stands crusted down the east side of trunk and branches with the white frost. The finishing touch.

But winter does not finish her. Spring always comes. The buds on the bare branches swell until they burst with blossom. Crisp and frilled and white, it clumps on the bare wood. This is my favourite cherry tree, oriental, mysterious. A strange contrast of tender blossom against calloused bark. This was the tree that sheltered that kiss.

It was one of those days that stand out from the jumble of childhood memories. Thinking of it now I can smell again the scones baking in the oven and the bread rising in the warming pans. Mother was baking. Tall and thin in her white apron, she dusted flour onto the scrubbed table top and pushed stray locks out of her eyes with the back of her hand. She was flustered from the heat and extra snappy. So, when the doorbell rang it was me who ran to answer it.

Euan McKay stood on the step, red-haired, freckled and sheepish looking to be caught doing an errand. He thrust two cardboard cartons towards me.

"I'm to fetch the eggs," he said.

Though we were in the same class at school I seem to think those were the first words he'd ever spoken to me.

"Who is it?" Mother called out, and added, " Will you close that door, I'm losing all the heat."

I nodded for Euan to come inside and pushed the door shut behind him. In the kitchen I put the egg cartons on the floured table top.

"Euan's here for the eggs," I said. Mother dusted more flopping hair from her brow and peered at him.

"Your mother's never ill, is she?"

Euan shook his head.

"No, we've got visitors." He looked at the floor as he answered and I felt a pang of sympathy seeing the flush rise on his cheeks and all but blot out his freckles. Mother banged the dough down on the table again.

"Well, I can't stop right this minute," she said. "Away out and play in the garden, the both of you. I'll give you a shout when they're sorted." It was a chore she would never let me see to, grading the eggs, and Euan's mother would want the largest.

The back door sucked more of the heat from the kitchen. Euan nipped out smartish. I stared at Mother's back, bent over the table, still slapping the dough and quite unaware of what she had done. A well of pure hatred bubbled up from my feet and burst over my head. The suddeness of anger riveted me to the step and froze my hand on the door knob. She had no notion of me at all. She did not see that my childhood was gone and I stood in the empty space between the years with all the attendant fears and anxieties. What was I to do with Euan in the garden. Play? We could hardly even look at one another.

My look should have shrivelled Mother and the dough to a black and burnt crisp. When it did not I slammed the door hard, in a petty attempt at revenge, and drew sour comfort from her imagined snort of annoyance. We walked away slowly, down the garden path. Though side by side there was a yard between us that might have been a mile. My nails cut into the palms of my hands.

For communication we made sidelong glances at each other when we were sure the other was looking away. Then a mistimed glance locked our eyes together. My mouth fell open expecting words to come automatically just as my fevered brain emptied of all sensible remarks. Euan, his eyes glued back to the ground, got some words to his tongue first.

"Samson was in a rotten mood on Friday," he said. Samson was our nickname for the Biology master, a big slab of a man whose voice was disturbingly shrill. We made a few more stabs at talk about school. None of it flowed with ease or intellect. My surge of hatred bunched up round my middle like skirts tucked in a child's knickers for paddling. Then we came to the tree. Euan gazed at the thick, crusty blossom.

"Hey," he said. "That's nice." His tone said more than nice so I sneaked a look at his face. The admiration for the cherry tree was plain to see. The ice was broken.

"Come inside." I ducked under the branches, stopping half way to let him know to follow. "See. Kind of Japanese, isn't she?"

He turned a full circle on his heels, looking round and up. As he completed the turn his head nodded agreement. Then we were embarrassed again, feeling the prison of the tree around us. I reached out and picked a bell from a clump of blossom, peering into it hard as if I'd never seen one before. I could have written a paper on its creamy smoothness, the crinkled lip, the pokered stamen, from the study I gave it. Euan also had a blossom in his hand when I finally looked towards him. Before I could turn away again, he reached out and tucked it in by my ear.

"Pretty," he said. Surprise made me look into his eyes. After a million years of being plain I wanted it to be me and not the flower. That was when he kissed me. I think it might have been as unexpected for him as it was for me.

His mouth was warm and dry and felt quite nice pressed against my own. The breath from his nostrils was somehow more hot and intimate than his lips. I wondered if I should lean against his chest or put my arms round him but they were trapped under his and I daren't move less I spoiled the moment. It was over all too soon. Euan dropped his arms and the space between us grew gigantic again. But our eyes held, his pale blue and steady, mine searching. I had a notion something should be said, something more should happen. But I did not know what.

Mother's voice cut between us, sharp as knives.

"Annie!" She shrieked. "The eggs is ready."

With a grimace at Euan, I crouched out from under the tree and walked back to the house. He kept a step or two behind me and I was glad of that. Inside the kitchen, Mother seemed more flushed than ever. She looked at neither of us, but waved the rolling pin at the egg boxes.

"I took the time," she snapped. "Your mother'll pay me later, I expect." Euan was dismissed.

I closed the door behind him, not sorry to see him go, and

went back to the kitchen. I had to go back to the kitchen. I couldn't have borne the indignity of being called down from my room which was where I really wanted to be just then. Mother flickered her eyes over me.

"I'll finish off in here," she said. She might have meant - I saw you under the cherry tree with that boy, or even - were you kissing him? I couldn't tell. I was just glad she didn't say the words that would ruin the memory. I hurried off to my room then to savour it, examine it, speculate and re-examine.

And Euan? Well, he made no mention of it to me. Not that year or the next. And by then I had an interest in another young man and had given up speculating as a way of life. The times when I noticed Euan look at me in school were only gilt to a memory that seemed to be mine alone and not his. Yet for all that, I think of him still with affection and warmth. It was quite the most poignant kiss I have ever shared.

The arrival of Archie Blair this afternoon had set me remembering. The cherry tree has developed rot in her roots and the bark flakes in handfuls from her trunk.

"She'll have to come down," he says. And goes off to fetch his saw.

When he re-appears at the back of the house, the children follow him down. They shriek at each other, vying for the right to shout "Timber". My husband shrugs at me and follows them, to watch and keep them out of harm's way. I retreat upstairs.

The sharp whine of the saw knives through the air. I can't imagine the garden without the cherry tree. Nor my bedroom window as an empty frame. Every event of my life is marked by one of her many moods. Teenage mopings, marriage, quarrels, childbirth - I've hung my memories on her boughs like baubles on a Christmas tree.

To avoid the window I stare into the mirror at my forty year old face. At the fine lines and the sprinkled grey in my hair. But it's the evenness inside that tells me spring will never come again. It's autumn now. The first fruitless autumn. The keening sound of the saw sings loud in my ears. In my head I can see the spinning blade with its shark teeth.

When the noise stops and I can make out the children's muted riot, I come back downstairs. Mother is seated by the fire. Her hair is quite white now, all over and not just dusted with flour. She asks me about the noise.

"It's Archie Blair," I tell her. "He's cut down the Cherry tree." She nods her white head. Her eyes don't look up at me.

"Tell him to burn it where it is," she says.

My mouth falls open, wordless again. I stare at her thin, shrunken form and wonder if Mother, too, has fastened memories on the old tree. Am I to discover now, after so many barren winters of yearning, some common ground, some shared emotion? The old ache opens wide as an axe welt inside me, eager and hungry, still, to be filled. Then, for a minute, her head nods up to look at me.

"The ashes will be good for the grass."

And I remember again, with perfect clarity, that white-hot sudden surge of hatred I felt that day, for her and for her ignorance of me.

THURTEENTH MEMBUR

Musnae be late. Cannae be late. Diana curse this daurk. The nicht o aw nichts. Cannae be late. Whit moved ower there? Some speerit - up tae nae guid. Tae mak me loss ma road. Ma amulit. Goat it. Fist in ma ticht fist, keepsafe. Diana, whaur's yer licht? Whit's that up there? Ach, naw. The fire's lit. Hope ah'm no late. No fur Samhein's Eve an me tae be brocht in. Ah'll rin. Ah'll rin. See, the shaddas. Is awbody here bit me? If - ah could - jist catch - ma braith -

Ehvoy!

Freends. Brithers, sisters. Aw ma freends. Sae guid tae me. Sae gled fur me. Ah'm gaunnae wurk. Wurk haurd. Ah needtae learn. Ah jist wish - naw, dinnae think aboot that. Jist aboot the nicht. Jings, ur we ready sae quick. Ma hauns ur wet, wi sweat. The Maister draws the circle. Fur us tae consecrate. Brither Leo, yer haun is strong in mine. Wid gie me courage. Ah could yaise some courage.

Dusk speerits an dawn, Day speerits an nicht, Come yin an come aw, come aw you that micht. Circle go roon, roon an aboot, guid speerits come in, eel speerits keep oot.

It's warum noo. The fire burns weel. A guid sign, sharely. Brither Teasle kens ah'm quakin. Minds his ain. Ah feel his sympithy. Och, ah could've telt him. He wid've helped. Whey, whey the Maister? Whey fur me? They must aw hear me shakin ower fire, watter an the chant. The chant!

Har, Har, Hou, Hou, danse ici, danse la, joue ici, joue la. Sabbat. Sabbat!

Noo it's begun. Diana, haud ma tongue. S'too late fur confeshun noo. Must step furrit. Must walk. Think oan the wurds, an whit ah'm tae dae. Richt haun - Athame. Left - the Penticle. Och Maister, there is kindness in yer face. Ah dinnae deserve it.

This nicht o Samhein ah turn ma back oan faith that shackles me tae men. Ah wullnae wurship daith bit life, an ask tae be brocht in tae wisdum through the craft.

Maister, an teechur. Must turn tae him. Gie homage wi the kiss. Fower times, the fower portals o life. It's done, done richt. An no sae hard. He seals me wi the mark. Caws oot ma name. Tara. Sister Tara. Aye, it suits me. Noo ah'm Tara. Um ah chainged? Made new? Oh, ah hoap so.
Ach, ah near furgoat. The talisman. He waits fur me tae take it. Gift o luck charm fur me. Ticht in ma haun ye stey till ah'm safe back in the circle. Ah wish we wur eatin noo, makin toasts an talk. An this wis dun wi. Ah cannae think. Think!
Ma sisters take ma cloak. Michty, it's no warum efter aw. Sister Alder's still it hur Black Fast. She's entranced. Here bit no here. A bit like me. He must still be weel - even yit. The man wha taen hur wean awa. Ah widnae be in his shune fur, by the goads, she frichtens me. Noo they waash me. Hope they dae it weel. At least the ile hus some heat in it. Feels guid.
Ha, whit wid ma freends think if they seen me noo. Shinin nakit

28

as a slug oan damp grund. Naw, they'd no make fun. No efter
Miss Mairshall. Great blisturs oan hur tongue, they say. Ah
made the spell tae pey her due. It fits. She should be mair
carefu whin she caws doon a freend o mine. Or buy hersell the
mano in fica, or weer blue beads. Pair Morag cannae help bein
slow.
They're feenished an me stull dreamin. The cup! An he's
annoyed. Ah see it in his een. Ah'm sorry, Maister. Ye taught
me weel. Ah'll git it richt, ah wull! Ah nearly drunk, furgoat the
prayer! The wurds, the wurds -

Woman wha guides the mune, Man wha guides the sun,
remake ma perfect sowl an gie me strength tae mak the flesh an
soul as wan.

Wull it be done? Ah hoap it's done. Ah nearly spilt the cup.
Tastes soor, bitter wi Mugwart, Periwinkle. Bit ah'm cleansed.
It burns ma throat, fires ma belly. Nearly done noo. Shin be
time tae dance, tae dance! Jings, ah'm reelin. Ma heid is spinnin
wi this drink. Whit ur they chantin? They're daen the roond
dance, sunwies - wurkin whit's guid. Bit that chant - soonds like
the invocation. Ma ears thrum, cannae hear. Wurk, wull ye?
Wurk!

We caw ye up this end o year, greatest speerit, jine us here.
Lit yer presence bring us licht, come an help us oan this nicht.

Naw! They cannae. Ah'll no listen, wullnae hear. Bit the wurds
rin through ma heid. Think aboot skil. Aboot Paul. Naw, no
aboot Paul. Whitever else, no him. Diana, dinnae heed. Keep
him by ye. They waant tae honour me bit wid show ma shame.
Och, whey did ah no confess it Beltane!
No the Auld Yin. No fur me. Maister. Maister, whey kin ah no
see? Lit it be you. You widnae ken. It least ye widnae care. An

ah could staun you mockin ma deceit. Bit the Auld Yin - cawed
fur me. Ah daurnae think!
Is that shadda? Hoarns - Him! Or the Maister, airms luftit, tae
drive the cone o pooer. Ah'll confess - if it's Him. Break the
spell. Hoo wull ah ken, hoo wull ah tell? Sister Catnip, she sayd
- telt me it esbat. Sayd he drives an ice cauld shaft. Aye, that's
it. If He comes - ah'll shout ma sin -brek the chant -
Is that a chill? Ice touchin me? Too late. Too late. It must be -.
Aw, Diana, mither o licht, make me vurgin fur wan nicht -

FOOTNOTE: deflowering with an artificial phallus was a Pagan custom much maligned by
later *women-controlling* religions where female sexuality was deemed dangerous and
assigned to the control of men by elevating, preserving and securing virginity. The term
virgin sacrifice was probably coined to denote male distress at, and church disapproval of,
women continuing with a custom which prevented the required proofs of virginity being
shown.

WANTING

Ellis needed a wife. He went in to tell Morag about it. Knees tucked well under the kitchen table, he stated his need. Morag would have the answer. Morag had solutions for every eventuality.

"What do you want a wife for?" She stirred the baking mixture more slowly and looked annoyed with him.

"Well -." Her annoyance shook him but he struggled on. "I can't do that -" pointing to the baking bowl.

"Heavens sake, Ellis. Here." The bowl was in his arm. "Stir."

He stirred, watching her take the apron off, shake it and hang it on the hook behind the kitchen door. This was going to be a serious conversation. He waited till she lifted the red kettle off the cooker. If she was going to make tea, it'd be safe to continue. She moved to the sink, planked the kettle lid on the draining board." Well, you see. I -" He didn't get any further. Morag turned on him.

"Oh, aye. I see all right. Your Mother's not cold in her grave and you're all of a sudden needing a wife. Oh, I see all right, Ellis Marshall." Water sprayed everywhere as she turned the tap on too hard, swore, and turned it back a bit. "And what, pray tell me, would a wife be wanting with you?"

He hadn't thought of it turned around that way and tried to

recollect his assets. Forty, round in the middle and thin on top. And slow, he knew he was slow. Morag could talk rings round him. Ever since they were in school she'd dazzled him with the number of words she could get out in one go.

"I've got the farm -"

"Farm? Farm!" He was shot twice and she never halted. "It was your Mother made that farm anything. She was the one with the head for figuring. She was the one with the orders. *Do this, Ellis. Do that, Ellis.* You were the one doing what she said. And a good job too, or there wouldn't be any farm today and most likely there won't be any farm tomorrow." She drew breath and slowed down. "Your wife would have to run the farm too."

He nodded. It was true, every word of it. Drive a tractor, he could do. Plough, plant, harvest, milk, feed the pigs, dip sheep and see to the hens. All of this he could do. It was a small mixed farm, self-supporting rather than profit-making, like most of the farms about. Turn his hand to anything practical, he could. Do anything except brain work. Buying, selling, planning, ordering, book-keeping - his mother had done all that. All that and the cooking. She had been a canny woman, his mother, if a bit short on patience with her slow-witted son.

Morag put a cake tin down in front of him.

"Pour that in there," she said. "Then pop it in the oven."

The next day she came up to the farm and showed him how to boil eggs for his lunch, and how to sew a button on his shirt. He stitched slowly, pulling the thread all the way out to arm's length. But he surprised himself. It was easy once you knew how.

"You'll have to get a machine," Morag looked at the pile of washing. "No, that one's no good." She forestalled his remark. "You want an automatic. And a drier. No woman these days is going to wash in that old thing." He got out the bank books and the cheque book. After the funeral, the lawyer had got everything changed to Ellis' name but he hadn't figured out how they worked yet. He put the books down on the table in front of Morag.

"Well - " she looked from the columns of figures to him. "I think we should just go down the town right now and buy them both." So that was what they did, going from shop to shop while Morag debated the pros and cons of various machines with the sales assistants. When it was finally settled which would suit him best, both machines were loaded onto the pick-up and he drove back to the village feeling strangely benevolent and pleased with himself.

"You can just wipe that smile off your face right now, Ellis Marshall," she said. "I'll have to arrange a plumber for you in the morning and if you keep on spending money at that rate, it won't matter how much you've got, it won't last long." Nevertheless, he kept right on smiling. These new machines fascinated him. He'd quite fancied the electric kettles too, and the shiny enamel cookers. He liked machines.

After Morag was away home, he sat down with the instruction leaflets and figured out that the washer just wanted a free supply of hot and cold water fitted. It was no harder than fixing and fitting pipes in the milking shed. He had it plumbed in before he went to bed and working, swishing away with him sitting watching it go round, sucking in water and spitting it back out again, when Morag arrived next morning, early to phone the plumber.

"Aye," she said. "We'll maybe make a husband of you yet." She was the one to know about husbands, Ellis thought. She'd had one for years, from not long after they left school up until a few years ago. Big, quiet man called Ben who used to come up and help on the farm during harvesting, for the fun of it. *To get away from the wife*, he used to joke. Not much of a joke now, Ellis realised. Ben had died of a heart attack three years ago.

"I'm away to my work," Morag said. "Come down about six

and we'll have supper." She worked in the paper-mill, making up the wages. Doing the paperwork. Ellis smiled at his little joke, got up from in front of the amazing machine and looked round the kitchen. He was learning something, the dishes were washed and stacked, vegetables were chopped and potatoes scrubbed for his lunch. He hadn't mastered the art of puddings, so he managed without, ate fruit and tightened his belt a notch. It was peaceful in the kitchen. Peaceful and sunny.

"I'll maybe get one of them hoovers," Ellis said. The dog looked up at him, cocking its head expectantly, the wall-eye bright in the sun. "Come on then, time to get on." The dog was at the door before he finished speaking.

That night he made the supper, following Morag's instructions to the letter. And it was good, pork chops with onions, a salad, new potatoes from the farm with butter and oatmeal on.

"Chops could have done a bit longer," Morag said, pushing her cleared plate away. "But you're getting there."

"Och, I don't know," he said. "I'm not as hungry as I was."

"Hungry? Hungry!" She had a habit of doing that, both barrels emptied and him wondering what he'd said wrong. "Is that all it is, then, Ellis Marshall? A cook is all a wife's for. Well there's other things, you know. Food's for needing. But there's wanting. Oh, aye, there's wanting too." She had got up and come round to his side of the table. Her eyes glinted and, involuntarily, he stood, hearing his chair scrape back. She put her hands on either side of his face and her mouth against his, moving her lips so that his parted. So he was kissing her right back and her arms went round his neck and her body came right up close against his so he could feel her breasts and her belly and her thighs press against him.

"There's wanting," she said, breaking off the kiss and coming back, hungry, to his mouth again. And he was wanting so much he was hardly aware of the struggle out of their clothes, or his nakedness, or even hers. He'd never seen a woman without clothes on, and he hardly saw now, for his eyes, like all the other parts of him, were burning. But he was doing it, doing it for all he was worth, for the first time in his life, and with Morag whom he'd known all his life. And he couldn't believe, and he was believing. He was hot, so hot, and exploding. Oh, exploding.

The second time, she told him to slow down a bit, and to touch her here and like this, and here and like that and to not be in such a hurry. And he did everything she said, and tried to do it exactly as she said he was to and it seemed to work though he wondered if she was going to die, the noise she was making, several times but she didn't and that was all right. So they did it again and he thought he was just getting good at it when the sun came up and he was going to have to go for the cows.

"And you'll still be needing your books keeping," she said as he stepped out into the morning.

He wasn't thinking about book-keeping. He was thinking about how it was right enough after all, people did it for it the fun of it. Not like the beasts, though it was hard to tell what the bull or a ram was thinking the dog always looked shame-faced, as if it didn't know why its body was jerking about like that and with its eyes trying to explain it'd much rather be chasing rabbits. But they kept right on doing it, mind, even though it didn't look a pleasure. He was half-way up Quarrybrae when he felt his jaws aching and put his hands up to his face to draw the grinning corners of his mouth down to a more comfortable set.

All day he kept finding his hand up at his jaw, trying to erase the smile that kept stiffening his muscles. And he kept stopping, just standing and not continuing what he was doing, while he grinned and was dunted several times by beasts wondering why nothing was happening quite with the same timing as they were used to.

In the afternoon, he took his grin and went down into the village for his papers and some groceries. In the paper shop when Jeannie Black turned to fetch the book for what he owed, he was looking at the curve of her breasts, her buttocks, the line of her thigh through her skirt. And when she turned round to him, and saw his eyes and the wide grin on his face and the fixed set of him, she turned red, bright red. He felt his own cheeks flush because she knew and they both stammered and muffed the exchange of his money, with his big, course hands becoming tangled with her fine, slim fingers and them both getting redder. And still he was smiling, smiling like he was simple and not just slow.

He went down to see Morag as soon as she would be in from her work. For once, he knew just what she was going to say and he was still wearing his smile.

"Can't keep away," she said, opening the door to him.

"I'll not come in," he said. "I've dinner on, for two."

"There's initiative." She was pleased with him, at last, and would be more pleased.

"I know who I'm wanting for my wife," he burst out. "Jeannie Black." And there was Morag, who was so like his mother, telling him what to do and how to do it, and giving him all this help so he could be fit for a wife, and she was screaming at him. Screaming at him and throwing things as he backed away from her, and hurried out the gate back up Quarrybrae, and he didn't know why because there was Jeannie, not much for the cooking, quiet and needing a man who knew what was what and whose hands when they touched his had told him she'd be all right about the wanting. And, oh yes, she'd be just great at the book-keeping too.

STEPPIN OOT

Ah only went oot fur a smoke. Honest tae goad. A smoke. That's aw. Bert's a pal o mine. So ah widnae. It's jist, weel ye kin see in thur windae fae the side o oor hut. An in the daurk, like. Wi thur licht oan. Ah wis jist staunin there, by the side o the hut, huvin a draw it ma fag.

Okay, so ah shoulda moved. Okay. Bit it's bin a while. An they couldnae see me, right? An ye dinnae expect - no wi yer neeburs an them mairrit years mair'n me. No in the kitchen. Wi the licht oan. Christ, ye try no tae think. Bin a long while.

So ah couldnae settle. Couldnae stey there, couldnae go in. Aye right, it hud goat tae me. That square o licht. Burnt in ma heid. That pitchur. Bit ah went fur a walk tae settle masell. It wisnae cauld. The moon wis comin up, big an bonny. Orange. Comin ower the chimney taps. Me in the empty streets, an the moon. S'aw richt.

It bein Thursday, an work the morra, near awbody's in thur beds. Hardly a sowl aff the last bus. Ah'm staunin it the shoap whin it comes up. Mindin ma ain. Listenin tae the quate, cept fur the bus. An Alice Barbour clackin ower the road as it roars awa. She's ower young fur me oneywey. No ma type. Lippy. Hard. A wean jist, bit hard awready. Christ Betty, Betty'd see hur ower the back. She's an airmfu, Betty. Roon in aw the richt places. An wi thick, wavy rid hair that catches the licht aff the fire. Een that open tae ye whin she luks up. Like ye surprised hur. Weel, bin a while, in't it. An efter Bert's ? Luk, ah nivir asked fur it. Ah'm staunin there, it the shoap, mindin ma ain. She comes ower.

"Goat a licht?" Cocks hur heid. She's goat blonde hair, cut shoart. Sherp nose. Ah take the matches oot ma poakit.

"Couldnae spare a fag?" She grins, cheeky like.

Ah gie hur wan, an licht it.

"Ye're ower young tae smoke," ah tell hur.

"Ye think?" She's in nae hurry. She stauns there, blawin smoke oot in a thin grey line. Watchin it.

"Aye," ah say. "Stunt yer growth."

She laughs. A while since ah heard a wummin laugh yon wey.

"Oh, ye think?" She says, shovin hur shouders back, showin me hur chist. Ach, she's young. Bit aw richt.

"Mibbe no," ah say. Ah'm lukin it hur tits shovin it that thin cloath. Christ, she's gein me trouble, an she kens it. Playin wi me. She steps furrit so's she's pressin oan ma airm. Pits hur mooth up close tae ma ear. Hur braith's warum. Wet.

"Waant a look?" She whispers it. An goes back twa steps intae the close, oot the street licht. Ah go tae.

She's staunin, heid stull cocked tae wan side, swayin hur hips a bit, lukin it me like she's stull sayin it *Waant tae see?* Ma fingurs feel thick roon ma fag, hurs playin wi the button oan hur blouse. Unfastenin it. She wets hur boatum lip wi hur tongue, shoves the strap aff hur shouder an pushes hur bra doon. Ah cannae move. Christ, ah cannae move.

She takes a draw it hur fag, then airches hur back furrit so's hur tits luft.

"Ye like lukin, din't ye?" She says. " Dae ye waant it?" An ah've goat it. Ma airm roon hur, turnin hur heid tae mine, feelin fur hur tongue wi ma ain. An hur tit wi its hard ticht nipple's pressin in ma haun. Christ, bit. Christ ! Ah loup awa wi a rid-hoat pain burnin the back o ma wrist, an hur yelpin:

"Whit the fuck ur ye daen? Ye've tore ma claes. Ma brithers'll kill me!"

Ah'm suckin whaur she stubbed hur fag oan me, the bitch. She's puen hur claes oan, puen the teir in hur blouse thegither.

"Ah nivir sayd ye could touch me, ya durty buggar," she says, an shoves by, heels clatterin oot the close an awa up the road. There's a taste o burnt hair an burnt skin in ma mooth. Tears in ma een. Bloody Barbours. Christ.

Betty's in hur bed whin ah git hame. Ah steer the coal. There's a rid, puckert patch o skin oan ma wrist. Stull nippin. So's ma heid. Made a ful o by a sixteen year auld lassie. Aye, bit ah wantit hur. Stull dae. Christ, whaur am ah comin fae. Ah'm lichtin a fag, tryin no tae think, whin ah hear the gate. Then the thump oan the door.

"Come oot, McDoanald, ur ah'll come in an git ye."

Ma skin shrinks, crawlin up ma back. It's the Barbours, in't it. Aye, bit ah've loaked the door. An that'll no stoap thum. He thumps again.

"Come oot, ya bastard." That's Bill. Andra'll be there tae. Christ, yin wid be enough. Ye dinnae mess wi the Barbours. Betty's hauf wey doon the stairs. The weans'll wauken oney meenut.

"Joe," she says, quate. "Whit's happenin?"

Ah think aboot gaun oot the back door. Oot the back an ower the fields. Bit whaur dae ye go, Christ. A place this size. The fist ootside thumps again. Three times.

Betty moves, hur hair's toosled fae the bed an she's drawin hur dressin goon ticht roon hur. Ah huv tae go noo, fur she'll go tae the door. Betty stauns doon fur naebody. Christ, whaur dae ye go. Him ur hur. Ah turn the loak, fling the door wide. Bill Barbour luks up it me, a heid shoarter'n me bit wi the shouders o a bul. Hauns like meat loaf. Andra's leanin oan the gate post. Waitin.

Bill jerks his thumb tae the street. Mannerly. Ye dinnae dae a fella ower oan his ain grund. Yin o the weans girns upstairs.

"Joe?" Betty's askin whit's gaun oan. Christ, there's naewhaur.

"S'awright," ah tell hur. An ah step oot an shut the door.

LONG HAUL

Rain hung across the Shap as he made the run down from Carlisle. Like a grey heavy curtain it spanned the valley. He hit it with a smack, felt it part round the cab, heard it drum on the roof. The daylight dulled to a yellow glow. Reaching forwards he flicked wipers and lights on. Mac didn't mind the rain. He felt good on the downhill run. All the way from Aberdeen and as many runs as a man could make in twenty years. But he still felt good.

It was a long time since they'd taken that sudden steep drop and run it smooth. A long time since he'd had to climb down the gears and sweat on it. But it was still downhill. It was still his rig leaping forward to bite on the grey asphalt as the ground dropped away in front. A longer, smoother, speedier descent with the frail dimpled crash barrier a continuous reminder.

He always took the run down the Shap on an empty stomach just before lunch. There was nothing like the keen edge of fear to sharpen up an appetite. Nothing like knowing there was twenty tonne of Swedish pine at his back and if it went bad he'd maybe, just maybe halt the cab. But he'd have a thirty foot trailer jack-knifed up his arse. And a load that would keep travelling on.

He picked her up outside the Tebay truck stop. She stood by

the access road. Bare-headed, impervious, rain making rats tails in her hair. So he broke his own rule. On a full tank and a full belly he thought - what the hell. First time in twenty year. In the cab she shook her hair like a dog. Water spat onto the back of his hand, left round blacker spots on the wheel. He felt good still.

"Where to?" His idea of a joke. She shrugged. But he'd known it wouldn't matter. She'd been on the road a long time. They all had.

"South," she said. He watched as she stuck a battered hold-all under her feet and raked in her pocket for fags. Then he swung back out into the motorway traffic. Maybe it was the rain had made him act generous. It thrummed still on the roof of the cab, closing them in. Pasted photographs over the windscreen smiled down at them. Madge - at the door of the house. The two boys. He nodded at the pictures.

"My kids." His voice seemed loud and the silence empty. She didn't offer her fags when she found them. She didn't seem to listen either. He wondered if she knew what it was like - having family.

"Kids?" She said. "Sure. I had kids." The match head crumbled, left bare stick and a pink streak on the side of the box. He slid a pack from the dash, tossed them to her.

"Wet," she said. The damp box was rammed back in the pocket of her sodden coat.

Funny she should have kids. His own two grinned down at him. Not often they grinned, except in photographs. Obligatory then. Madge was grinning too. He didn't see much of them. Not on the road. Not with the house to pay for. Maybe he shouldn't have mentioned them. It was kind of uncomfortable to have them in the cab, grinning. Made him feel a queer need to explain, apologise. Funny she should have kids too.

"Exeter," he said. "That's where I'm headed."

"Fine." She blew a thin stream of smoke at the windscreen

and watched it spread across the glass. Strange kind of life, he thought, just travelling up and down the roads. Everywhere someplace you'd been and nothing to go back for. He was curious.

"Someplace special is it? Down South?" She looked at him then. First time since she'd got in the cab. Her eyes were grey - like the rain. She could have been any age.

"Land's End." She made it sound like nowhere. It was his turn to shrug. Land's End was for tourists. For long haired weirdos with back packs or bikes. Doing it for charity. He turned his attention back to the road. They were running out of the rain. It had thinned to a fine drizzle. He gave the lights to an overtaking container and settled down for the afternoon run. But it wasn't the same. Irritation prickled in his shoulders. The smell of damp clothes drying out filled the cab. He should have left her stand in the rain with her silence and her unconcern. Now he was shut in, cramped by the physical presence of her. She ought to know the ropes, ought to at least talk.

His eyes flicked back to the photographs. There was no comfort for him there. Mr Money was all he was to the kids. Think of them, think of their wants. And Madge. He wasn't sure anymore what he was for Madge.

"For them is it?" Her voice startled him. "For them," she repeated. "Long distance. For the money?"

"Oh. Yeh." He nodded the lie. The grey eyes were on his face. He corrected himself, sheepish to be caught out. "Hell, no. Guess I just like it."

"S'a good enough reason. For anything."

He eased his foot back, shook his head as a station wagon cut in too close, too soon. First of the blips, rushing to be home.

"The only thing," he said.

"Only thing you like? . . . Or the only thing you do?"

"Both," he said. He'd caught it from her. He must've caught it from her. Christ, she should still be at Tebay.

"Stupid Bastard!" He yelled, laying on the horn to make up for the one he'd let go. The blip that had tried the bumper swop slacked off then picked up speed. He eased back on the pedal. There'd be no race'n chase. It wasn't his style. But he could play her game. He didn't have to talk. It was his rig. Miles of grey road dashed under his wheels, heading North. His shoulders felt stiff. The seat didn't fit his back anymore.

"Been driving long?" She asked.

Another driver would have answered the hours for that day. But he was proud of his twenty years. He'd chalked them up one by one. With enthusiasm at first, then steadily and now he worked towards what he held as a triumph. Twenty five years on the road. It was a target like a date ringed with red on a calendar. A target he reached for with a feeling of glee.

So he forgot he had meant to stay silent and he talked. As he talked all his pride in his skill shone on his round face. He talked of his rig as a lover would talk of his woman. He exulted in the power under the boards and his control of it. The throb of the engine, the hiss of air from the brakes, a thirsty tank gulping diesel, the sing of tyre on tar - these were the things that put music in his life.

The woman's grey stare stayed on his face as he talked, watching his eyes. He staggered over sudden shyness.

"You'll be thinking I'm soft in the head."

"No, no," she protested. "I think you're lucky. To be so alive."

They laughed together - as though they shared some illicit secret. Mac felt himself spread out to fill the cab again. And he told her stories from years ago. Long and short. Sad and funny and strange.

The road ahead shrank to the beam of the headlights. Beyond was a black gullet lined with lighted teeth. Just south of Stafford he took the slip road at Junction 13. It was coming close on dinner time and he avoided eating in the giant service stations that straddled the motorway like modern dinosaurs. He liked the closed-in warmth of the Transport Cafe survivors.

He pulled onto the ash-park at Kate's Kitchen and let the engine growl twice before he switched off. A habit he passed off as feeding fuel to the carburettor for an easy start. But he knew he just liked to leave with the roar ringing in his ears.

"Dinner," he said. She climbed down and tugged the hold-all free from under her seat, joining him as he walked to the lighted cafe.

Inside Kate's the air was heavy with the smell of constant frying and tasted of bacon fat. Eggs spat on the griddle. The round tables were covered with plastic gingham cloths, yellowed at the edges, and set with salt and pepper, vinegar and squeezy containers of brown sauce that were never quite clean. In one of the side booths he caught sight of Big Ben with the Fixer tucked in beside him. The woman followed a step or two behind so that he had to stand aside to let her squeeze in at the table first. The other two drivers glanced at her and Big Ben nodded but they paid her no more attention than that.

"Thought they'd pensioned you off," he said to the Fixer. Fixer looked seventy, thin and lined.

"Naw," he said. "Been trying deliveries but nothing doing. Got to feeling like a yo-yo on a short string."

"We'll pass a coffin trundling North one o' these days," Big Ben grinned. "Be him!" His whooped laugh disturbed the greasy air and his broad shoulders shook heavily so that the table rattled. The young girl who'd come over to take their orders yawned her boredom.

Mac recited his list from memory. It read like the entire menu. The biggest meal he ate all day and it never varied. The girl made quick pencil marks on her pad then waited, tapping the pencil stub like a drumstick on the paper as she glanced at the woman.

"Just tea," the woman said. Mac screwed his head round.

"You'll have the same as me," he said. He screwed back to the girl. "She'll have same as me." The girl ticked out a two and walked off. Beside him Mac felt the woman shift in the seat.

"I'll get it," he said. She didn't reply. Ben coughed. Mac felt his spine begin to prickle. "Hell, you have to eat," he justified himself.

A pall of discomfort had crept up on him and touched them all. Then Fixer launched into one of his long tales. This time about short haul which made a change and took the scunner out of Mac's back so he felt easy with them again, like usual. When the food came he dove at it hungrily. The woman was hungry too and ate almost despite herself. He felt pleased then. Let them think what they liked. Just because you broke one rule. Didn't mean you had to change your life.

The Fixer gave a short foxy laugh.

"And d'you remember coming in through that door, Mac, with your handbrake in your hand." He slapped his knee and chuckled. "You want to have seen his face, Ben. A picture it was, a picture."

Mac grinned through a mouthful of food. That was the first time he'd met Fixer. And the time he'd learned where he got his nickname.

"Bloody lucky you was here," he said. The Fixer accepted the compliment as due.

"We were all held together with string in them days," he said.

"String and wire and a helluva lot of luck." Ben stood up. He towered above the table.

"I'm off," he said. "Before the violins start. See you." The Fixer rose to follow him out.

"Me an' all," he said. "I've sat my spell. Mind how you go, Mac." Mac nodded. He'd run into them again, a week, a month, a year from now. He sipped at his black stewed tea and watched the woman push her empty plate away.

"You was hungry then?" She nodded.

"Haven't ate much last couple of days."

Outside he checked the ropes for slack, tightening where it was needed. He worked steadily, content now he was fed and could rest up. The ropes were wet and stretched as he pulled on them. He worked up from the driver's door towards the rear. As he came round from the back he saw her leaning against the nearside door. Despite the dark he could feel the grey eyes on him. His spine tingled again. He loosed off the rope and pulled on it.

"I stop over now," he said. "Down the road a bit. You might pick up another lift here. If you wait on, like." He tied off the rope, not looking at her. He could tell she hadn't taken her eyes off him. His fingers felt like thumbs.

"S'all right."

He moved down to the last rope. Beside the cab where she stood. He'd noticed in the cafe her hair had dried and curled round her face. The wet rope was stubborn under his fingers. He stifled the irritation that grew in him.

"You can if you like," she said.

He looked at her then. Her face was close to his. So close he could make out the dark pupils in the greyness of the irises. But her look stayed with his. He had to turn away. He was having trouble tying the rope back.

"For the dinner," she added. He shook his head.

"You don't owe me," he said. He slapped the wet loop home, walked past her round the front of the cab and climbed in. The passenger door clicked open. Her head, then her face, then her body was back sliding into the seat beside him. He relaxed. On his home ground now, the wheel under his hand, leather at his back. His eyes flicked up to Madge's photograph over his head.

"Besides," he said. "No offence like. But how'd I know if you're clean." He could just hear Madge if he had to explain he'd given her something. Jees, she made enough fuss if he spilled fag ash on her good carpets. The picture was unbearable.

He blotted it out and switched on the engine. Unaware, the corner of his mouth smiled at the growl of the throttle.

A few miles down the road he drew into a lay-by and switched off again. It was black outside. Into the sudden silence fell the song of the motorway. On the right of them it rose out of the ground, pegged on concrete stilts. Passing lights whined through the night. He liked to sleep where he could hear it.

Inside the cab he clicked on the light. Reached for the newspaper. He was hardly settled when the first drops of rain spattered on the roof. It had caught up with them. He could tell from the size of the drops it would be a downpour. In minutes it thrummed on the cab. The windscreen became a waterfall. He could hear the drip, splash, drip from under the trailer over the skittering sound of rain bounced high off the tarmac.

Beside him the woman shuffled in her seat, searched in her hold-all. She was changing her clothes or some such thing. He clawed his attention back to the newspaper. Then the door clicked open. Rain spewed into the cab. He glanced over, past the humped towel that crouched on her empty seat. Saw the flash of her naked back as she dropped to the ground. Heard her gasp as the rain stung on her skin. The cab door slammed shut on the night again.

The newspaper crumpled in his lap. He caught sight of her, white and exposed, slip down the bank into the field beyond. On the grass she made a quick scan round. Then she raised her arms to the sky. And turned her face up to the rain. He knew she must have her eyes shut. The force of the rain would feel like the cut of a thousand steel spines on her flesh. His fingers raised of their own accord to wipe the mist of his breath from the window. Quite unaware, he hunched over her seat and the waiting towel to watch. He felt as though he gazed on some primeval rite of worship. Awed and amazed.

Now her hair streamed with water. She began to wash herself. Soap frothed in the hair of her armpits. Rain washed it away.

She soaped over her breasts, her stomach, her thighs. White bubbles collected in the dark patch below her belly before the rain rushed them, scudding down her legs. Then she hurried back to the cab. She reached for the towel left on the seat. Buried her face in it. Moaned and trembled with the chill of the rain.

Mac could not turn away. It took some conscious effort to raise his jaw-bone and close his mouth. He swallowed hard on the immovable lump in his throat. When she looked out of the towel, her eyes met his. He knew from the way they crinkled at the corners that her mouth, hidden under the towel, was smiling. Even though she trembled and her teeth chattered. She rubbed the towel over her breasts and her legs. But her eyes, greyer than ever and candid, never left his.

"I'm clean now," she said.

Her skin was cold, pimpled with goosebumps but her mouth was warm and hungry on his. Her nipples tasted of soap and the rain and she arched up against him drawing heat from his skin as he dragged the clothes off him with her helping as well she might. The cabin steamed and the windows fogged but Mac was back on the downhill run where it swept him along and sucked him down and his gut was shoved back to his backbone and fear curled high in his stomach. It was long and slow and sudden and frightening. And from nowhere it reached him. The dream of a sudden steep drop. It waited still. And he drove headlong towards it.

It was the whine of the motorway Mac heard first. It started to jump about seven. Blips on a heart monitor - speeding up. Sounding faster and faster to become a continuous solitary shriek. Fear dried his mouth and he woke. The seven thirty song settled itself steady in his ears. Then he heard the birds and her breath. The weight of her leg across his reminded him.

She was still asleep, looked younger asleep. Sometime they must have gotten onto the bunk behind the seats. They were cramped together. He would not be able to move without waking her. He knew this was going to be one of the big embarrassing moments of his life. He eased his leg from under hers and reached for his shirt. He had his head in it, poking out the top when he knew she was awake and saw the same grey eyes as yesterday, like she was dead already, looking steady at him.

"Time we was off," he said, squirming into his trousers under the blanket and thankful that he could dodge over into the driving seat before she spoke. He had the rig out, swung round the roundabout and bowling into the motorway traffic before she climbed down in front beside him. He was easy now. He was home.

"Them kids you said you had," he looked over at her. "You just up and leave 'em?" She was staring out the windscreen.

"I said my goodbyes." The grey eyes were fixed on the glass. Behind it was the pall of smoke, the flash of fire. And the charred black flesh on the grass under the blanket she had ripped aside. The scream of the traffic froze her. She couldn't remember who had screamed. But it went on, and on. Even with her hands over her ears, it went on. She shrugged, smiled with her mouth towards Mac's face.

"I said my goodbyes."

He wished he could. He looked up again at the prisoned smiles of his sons. At Madge. Her lips were parted a little, showing her teeth, like they were bared. They made him feel tired. An intruder in his own home. The perpetual lodger. And because she was still, and quiet, and contained, he began to tell her about them.

"Maybe you should stay home," she said after a while.

"That would be nice," he scorned. "That would be great. Mend this, fix that, mind your feet, move your butt. Give us a pound, give us a lift." His breath steamed down his nostrils. "Maybe they'd appreciate me!"

"Maybe," she said. It was a question. He didn't know the answer. Someday he'd have no choice but find out. But not yet, not for a while yet.

They had breakfast at Bristol. It was a meal Mac never liked. He was always eager to be up and off, back on the road while the day was fresh. He'd gotten quite used to having her in the cab. Her quiet spells, when she stopped listening or seeing him, didn't trouble him now. He just rolled back into being alone with himself and his rig. It was good to be comfortable and think his own thoughts. This was the last leg of his run and he soaked up every good mile of it.

The sun had come up with the morning. Grey fields became green. Colour picked out roofs and houses. By the time he turned off the M5 for Exeter the road was dust dry under his wheels. Up ahead was the junction. And the Plymouth road. He pulled the rig over and pointed.

"That's the A38," he said. "To the left. I go straight on." He watched as she tugged the hold-all from under the seat. It caught and she twisted in the seat to pull it free. Then she had it in her hands and was reaching for the door catch.

"You could stop on," he rushed the words out. "Get me back up the road." The door was open. A smile ghosted across her mouth.

"We're going different roads now," she said. Then she jumped. He was looking at blank space. At the empty field beyond. He leaned over, gaped out the open door at the top of her head.

"Hey," he shouted. "What the hell are you going to do at Land's End?" Her face turned up to him. The grey stare froze on his eyeballs.

"Jump off," she said. The door slammed shut.

He had to stop at the lights. In the mirror he saw her trudge down the Plymouth road a way, prop up the hold-all and sit down on it. When the lights showed green he roared the rig straight through. Crazy woman, he thought. Real crazy. There was nothing to make of her at all. But he had his peace back. The cabin was his own again. He kept his eyes away from the passenger seat that rode empty side by side with him all the way into Exeter.

He parked up in the woodyard, had his sheets signed and left them to unload her. It was hot now, the sun high in the sky and lunchtime. He settled for a beer at the first place he run across. Exeter reminded him of Aberdeen. Only wider and warmer. More foreigners too.

He remembered one time he'd gone in the pictures, the big cinema on the main street. A crowd of them had sat down in the row behind. They might have been French or Dutch. It was all Greek to him. They'd chattered away through the film, laughing at the jokes they'd discovered on the sides of the matchboxes. One of them had tapped him on the arm, passed the box over for him to read. It wasn't a very funny joke. They'd thought it hilarious. He wondered if they'd laughed with him or at him.

He swallowed the watery beer. There were always groups of foreigners on Exeter's streets. Might have been students at the University. Maybe just tourists. He left the last inch in the glass, it had no taste anyway, and went back for his rig. He'd make time and catch lunch up the road. The beer had sickened his appetite.

He drove out of town through the wide streets, round the green parks. Back the way he had come. The space in the cab beside him yawned wide and empty. Had she gotten a lift yet? He didn't see the road anymore. He saw her in the field. In the rain. And afterwards, she had clung to him like he was life itself. Madge never came on to him like that. His knuckles whitened on the wheel. Maybe she'd still be there, sat on her hold-all, waiting.

The junction was up ahead. The lights were going to red. His mouth tasted of soap and the rain. He braked up and looked down the Plymouth road. The space where she'd sat was empty. But she'd not have gone far. Nobody went all the way to Land's End. Nobody.

He glanced up at the pictures above his head. His sons sneered. Madge snarled. And his rig was in the wrong lane. His hand whipped out at the photographs - tore them down. He ripped them through and through. The cabin closed round him. He wasn't going anywhere. It was the road that moved. He dropped the torn pieces out the open window. Green shone on his face. He slammed in the gear, swung the rig over. A horn honked. The artic strained. It was a long haul back to Scotland and Aberdeen. And uphill all the way. In the wake of his wheels littered pieces of photograph danced in the dust.

LAST INJUN

"Ah'm no gaun."

She turns fae the sink an luks it me.

"Hoo d'ye mean, ye're no gaun." Hur face is weerin its *didnae unnerstaun ye* luk.

"By steyin in the hoose. By no gaun oot the door. That's hoo." A sixties disco, Christsake. Nae wey.

"Bit, Tam," she's wheedlin. "It'll bring back memries." Aye.

"Aye. It'll dae that aw right." Ah'm tryin tae git through tae hur. Wastin ma braith. She gits oan wi peelin the tatties.

"Ah've irened yer shurt. An ah pressed yer troosurs. Bill n'Irene ur gaun."

Whey dis she nivir hear me? Whey dis irenin ma shurt an pressin ma troosurs make me invisible? Mibbe if ah go aboot nakit she'll see me. Mibbe if ah stoap talkin aw thegither she'll hear hoo quate it is. Aye. Mibbe.

The Welfare Hall's fair loupin wi rackit. Irene waves us ower fae a table hauf wey doon the faur side. *Love me do* is beltin oot an there's twa young yins oan the flair awready, by thursells, gien it whit.

"Bill's gittin thum," Irene says. Ah go through tae the baur. Chainged days, eh. There's is miny wimmin gittin drinks is men. Bill's glowin awready. Twa dances an he'll luk like an ice lolly left in the sun. Meltit.

"You tak these twa." He gies me Maisie n'Irene's. Wan gin an tonic. Wan sweet martini. Nivir chainges. "Be a guid nicht," he shouts is we walk intae *Puppet on a String*. "Takes ye back, eh?"

"Aye." Sandie Shaw. Ah yaised tae fancy hur sumthin rotten. Maisie hud hair like that. Daurk, long. Straight. Widnae suit hur noo.

"Ta," she says whin ah pit hur drink doon, though it's a maitter o lip readin. Wan thing ah'm share o. They recurds wur nivir that lood whin we played thum. Thirty years. Ach, Maisie. Wance ah wantit awa fae here. Ah wantit higher hills, a lochside, mibbe the sea curvin roon rock, singin me awauk, sighin me tae sleep. Wance ah wantit tae tak photiegraphs. Wantit tae see if ah could make it. A stupit dream, she cawed it. A waste o time. Ach, ah shoulda steyed it hame.

Bit the whisky's warmin. Ah git a saicund roond in kinna quick an ah dinnae miss the sideweys luk fur aw she kens ah've nivir hud mairn'n twa whiskys thegither since afore the lassies wur born. Last disco ah wis it wis whin oor Shona goat mairrit. The thurd yin settled. Last o the Injuns, ah telt hur.

"That's whey we're whoopin it up, Da," she sayd.

"C'moan," Maisie gits tae hur feet. Bill's goat a hud o Irene an he's singing *Teddy Bear* alang wey the song, his vice twa octaves deeper'n usual, tryin tae soond like the King. Jist is weel it's daurk in here. There's fower stane hingin aboot him wisnae there in the sixties. Aye, an ah'm nae chookie burdy masell. The slippery slope. So ye check roon, dint ye? Checkin the damage.

Near awbody in the place is here. Bert luks helluva pale wi the coal stoor waashed aff. Meg fae the post oaffice is gien it laldy. Guid dancer. Furst time ah've seen hur legs fur years. Must mind an gie hur a dance efter ur she'll no lit me furget it. Ay yin tae bear a grudge, is Meg.

The record chainges tae *Saturday Night at the Movies* an Maisie's no fur sittin doon. She grins it me. Ah want tae tell hur no tae dae that bit ah grin back. Oh, ah mind aw right. Sittin in the back raw. Oh, ah mind. Bit ah cannae feel it oney mair. Ah jist mind whit it felt like then. Aw that waantin, hoat, like ye hud a feevur. Hur an all. Vanished fur aw time efter she hud oor Shona. Taen a year or twa tae knock it oot o me, bit. Wunner if she minds whit it felt like.

Bill n'Irene gie up furst. There's anither whisky waitin oan the table whin we git there. Maisie luks it me sideweys again. Ah lit it lie, tak Irene up fur the Twist. Ken, ye dinnae furget, dae ye. *Like we did last summer*. Micht hae been, right enough. We're showin aff noo and the ithers ur gein us boady room. Life in the auld dug yit.

The music slips intae a smoochy wan. Irene snuggles up tae me, pits her mooth against ma ear.

"Guid thegither, in't we." She says, an hooks hur thumb intae ma troosur belt. Life in the auld dug, right enough. She noads hur heid it Rab Connell an Betty McIndoe. Supposed tae be a big secrit bit ye'd need tae be blund. This year, them. Next year somebody else. Only, it'll no be me. Ah'll no be markin Irene's caird fur hur. Be jist like Maisie wi diffirent claes oan. An that's bin deid fur years. Stull, wan thing. It micht be deid bit it's no drapped aff yit.

Ah dinnae git tae sit doon. Maisie's goat a haud o ma airm. It least, it luks like Maisie. Feels like a vice.

"Ye waant awbody talkin aboot ye," she hisses oot the side o hur mooth. "Waant tae make a laughin stock o me. Like, like John McIndoe or Jean Connell." Weel, ah try.

"Maisie, we wur dancin. That's whit we come here fur. That's whit we're daen."

Ah dinnae think ah spoke.

"You huv me talked aboot in this place," she says. "An you wull be sorry. Very sorry." Her mooth's like a streeched gutty band, an thur's a tick jumpin at the edge o hur ee. She's dancin awa like there wis nuthin wrang and ah ken tae the exact inch hoo mad she is. Ah'm lukin furrit tae a week o breed an watter an the *huv ye noticed hoo heavy it is* silence.

Ah'm thinkin ah'm awready sorry. Ah've bin sorry fur the last thurty years. That moarnin, staunin in the back kitchen, dressed fur the kirk an waitin fur Bill tae fund the ring, ah wis sorry. Ah stuid lukin it the trees marchin up the brae an ootae the village an kent ah should stoap it there an then. Couldnae dae it, bit. Couldnae pluck up the courage.

Bit ah thocht ah'd dun aw richt by hur. Ah kep workin, kep oor feet clear, hoose an weans weel seen tae, gied hur awthin she wantit. Noo, she's dancin like a stick in front o me, lettin oan awthing's fine, jist fine, fur the sake o awbody else in the hall. An hatin me. That line o hur mooth streeches back thurty year. Christsake, ah did neethur o us oney favurs. Ah stoap dancin.

"Ah'm gaun hame," ah tell hur. She stares it me.

"Ye cannae. Ah've the raffle tae dae efter." She's weerin that 'didnae unnerstaun ye' luk again. Then she dis it. Luks roon tae see if oneybody hus noticed. An ah hate hur like ma hert burst wi it, rid an explodin in ma chist, ma belly, ma heid.

"Ah'm gaun." It's aw ah daur say though ah waant tae vomit oot years o it. Ma joab that wis nivir guid enough, the dreams she made a ful o, things ah did in the hoose that wur aye wrang, the gairdin nivir plantit wi whit she wantit whin she wantit it, wanes that goat ma charactur gein thum week efter week, year efter year. An every memry's a step oot the hall an up the road awa fae hur. A bag's aw ah'm needin, an sum brass. Somewhaur, the sea is dancin oan rock an the hills staun roon like wawfloors. Ah'm gaunnae huv the kinna silence that talks tae ye, even if it's too late. Even if it kills me. If ah hurry, ah'll jist catch the last bus oot.

YOSEPH

Yoseph was a big man with swollen fore-arms and beefy jowls and a bald head with a crest of thin fair hair dusted round the shining crown. He always wore an apron, white but stained with dirt from the potato sacks, green from the cabbages or smudged with brown that might have come from the bananas. He looked like a butcher rather than a grocer and, if he'd acted as appearance suggested, would have laughed a lot and been jolly with his customers. But Yoseph never laughed. He talked slowly and seriously, always about business and always in broken English. He was Polish and had come to the village after the war, opened the shop and become naturalised.

"I Scottish," he would say, if anyone referred to his nationality. "Yoseph," he would correct, if anyone decided his name might properly be Joseph and called him so. Whatever, his shop was named by the villagers as *The Pole's* and if a stranger asked was he in the Pole's, Yoseph answered yes. He knew the value of a business identity and never used two words if one would do.

The shop was bright and clean and because of that, busy. Yoseph was always sweeping and wiping, whenever he wasn't serving, slicing meat or cheese or carrying through sacks of vegetables or flour from the back shop. His measure was always exact, the sliced meat a precise quarter, the mince an exact pound. He was masterly with the wire cheese cutters.

"Six ounces you want?" Six ounces you got. Even Isa Cameron had a grudging respect for him.

"That lassie in the store disnae know a quarter o ham means a quarter o ham and no three an a half ounces," she grumbled, putting the freshly cut six ounce of cheese in her basket. "You don't do nobody, Yoseph. Mind, you don't do nobody no favours, either." The latter gripe about a possible sliver extra in case the scales weren't set quite right fell on deaf ears. Yoseph took Isa's money, gave her change and nodded impassively as he turned to the next customer. "Mean as they come," Isa muttered on her way out the shop. "As soon crack an egg as a smile."

But that's how Yoseph was. Dependable, stolid. And with Yoseph it went deep down. He didn't mix, never shared information about his life, past or present. His impassive front went all the way round. A coat with no fastening. Not like Maisie Paine. No, not at all like Maisie Paine. She's a woman of appearances. Everything was always hunky-dorey with Maisie. In the street, her weans could do no wrong. But you'd hear her screeching at them from inside her house even from across the road. Her man, to listen to her, was the great provider, the soul of generosity, would never express an opinion at odds with hers let alone act without her approval. Until the night he left, of course.

That was five years ago. We were all coming up the road from the Welfare Hall that night, from a sixties disco, a crowd of us. Not noisy, but happy. And there was Maisie. She came tearing out of the back road into Main street and stopped at the bus stop. Stopped isn't quite right. She was like a wild woman. Pacing. Back and forth, onto the road, back to the pavement. A look up the road, a look down. And all the while a thin sound trickled out of her mouth. The last bus was long gone.

After that, she never had a good word to say of him and

would take every chance to re-tell what a bastard he was, all his life. All his life. The only thing that put a smile back in her eyes was her granddaughter. Lucy was a bonny bairn and, of course, being Maisie's granddaughter, slept through the night from the off-set and was light years ahead of all other bairns in everything.

She was up visiting again today, Lucy. Nearly five now and with her blonde hair dulling to fair. Maisie had her out in the street, showing her off.

"I put the plaits in her hair," she said. "Well, she suits it, and it only gets knotted up otherwise. Our Shona had it in two bunches but I told her, it'll only get knotted up like that. Plaits are much tidier."

The little girl stood solidly beside her grandmother. She was wearing a print dress with a Spanish frill.

"I made it," Maisie boasted. "Just like one I made for her mum. They'd have them all in jeans these days but I think a wee girl doesn't look like a wee girl unless she's in a frock."

We were outside the Pole's. Three or four of us, Maisie and me on our way in and the others on their way out. Certainly, it was weather for a dress. Sharp sunshine glinted off the shop windows, on the silk ribbons in Lucy's hair. Yoseph came out with the window pole to pull the shade down a bit. His shop has changed some in the past forty years, kept up to date with pre-packaged, processed and frozen food. But Yoseph hasn't changed. His bald head shone. He was middle-aged when he came to the village and he's middle-aged now.

"Aye, you're not keeping the sun out when we get this little of it, Yoseph," Maisie said.

He had the pole hooked in the eyelet of the shade, easing it down, when he glanced over his shoulder. His expression changed as he turned. The response never emerged from his opening mouth. He stared. He let the pole drop away from him towards the window and hang there, hooked in the eyelet, swinging. His whole solid body wavered.

"Anna!" He said. Then he moved. In one flowing shift he was on his knees in front of little Lucy, his arms round her, the child vanishing into the bulk of his arms and chest. "Anna," he cried. "Anna, Anna!"

The girl had been jerked from her grandmother's grasp and Maisie, like the rest of us, stood, inert and unable to assimilate anything. Then she recovered her animation, slapping at Yoseph's head, pulling at his shoulders.

"You let her go," she screamed. "You get your dirty hands off that wean." She kept it up, a stream of blows and obscenities as Yoseph, startled, first tried to protect the child and then, perplexed, loosened his grip and had Lucy torn free of him by her demented granny.

"I'll get the police to you," Maisie screeched, gripping Lucy's placid hand and dragging the bemused child over the road and away towards home. "You men are all the same. Touch my grandwean, would you. I'll have the police to you."

I turned towards Yoseph, still on his knees with his empty arms bent, still open and his eyes full of puzzlement and something that might have been pain. I moved forward, embarrassed at being there, wanting to put out my hand, to help him up but he stumbled to his feet and turned up the shop step without seeing me. Behind me the others shuffled away. I followed Yoseph up the step but he pushed the door between us.

"Shop shut," he mumbled. "Shop shut." The door closed and I turned away, cold in the sunshine, ashamed and out of place in my village. The window pole still swung, tapping gently on the glass.

HOMECOMING

The noise woke her. A deafening, solid thump. Then the screaming. It was the wrong time to be asleep. Now, peeling the potatoes, she could see half sink, half black. One side of her face was hot and numb. Every now and then blood dropped and spread in the muddy water.

The food cooked. Needing to be properly awake, presentable, she washed her face in cold water. The towel felt hard. Her left eye was still seeing black. When the doorbell rang, nobody moved. He had forgotten. Then he remembered and answered it. Standing in the kitchen, with the door closed, she heard the conversation.

"Gerry, come in, come in! What can I do you for?"

"I want you to come to a meeting tonight. It's important. Four of the top brass'll be there. Time we said what the local Branch want. You should be there."

"Right. Sounds good. Right." She waited, listening, knowing what would come next. "Ah, but Karen goes out on a Thursday. Her art class." He was considerate, though despondent. Then he brightened some. "Unless she's not fussy about going tonight. I'll see what she's planning."

He opened the kitchen door, put his head round. "Hey love, it's Gerry. Wants me to go to a meeting. You going to your art group?"

She looked at him, brightly lit from the strip lights down one side, shadowy down the other. His eyes were clear, questioning. She stared and said nothing.

"No?" He said. "Oh, but that's not fair. You only go out one night." He vanished into the livingroom. The door closed. "Look, leave it till later, Gerry. If I'm there, I'm there. Okay?"

The outside door shut. There was a tattoo of sound crashing against wall, door, table, chair. It broke on her, screaming again. She went down under it, swept away by it, drowned in it. When she surfaced, she served dinner. The boys ate quietly. She had to hold her chin with one hand and spoon soup in the corner of her mouth. Something had cracked. Swallowing was difficult. He talked.

"I should go tonight. National Secretary, huh. We don't often get the chance." He looked at her, waiting for an opinion.

"You should go, then." The words sounded slurred. They were the wrong words. The crash brought tears from Derek. The screaming swallowed them all. When it subsided, he took Danny's pork chop, ruffling the dark hair with his other hand.

"You don't want it anyway, do you son?" He smiled at her, justifying. "He'd have eaten it by now."

She cleaned up the boy first. Cold water, a pad on his nose. As much love and hugging as she could squeeze into the operation. Danny sat motionless at the table. She picked him up, washed him too, put them both to bed. It was seven o'clock.

He was singing in the bath. *The Longest Day*. Blood, sweat and tears. She cleaned the splashes of blood off the kitchen wall first, scraped the beans and bits of pork from the door, the window, the floor, put the broken plate in the bin. The hot water stung her hand.

He appeared behind her, wrapped in a towel, whistling.

"Yeh," he said, slapping on aftershave, peering past her into the mirror. "Knock 'em dead, eh?" He looked at her warped reflection, pressed up against her and slid an arm round her waist. "How about a quick one before I go? Ever ready, that's me." He laughed.

She felt his erection stiffen against her buttocks and took her hands out of the water. There were four even red holes on the right one that puzzled her. When he was satisfied, she went back to washing the dishes. He dressed watching her.

"What are you going to do tonight? Paint?" She nodded and he left, banging the door behind him, whistling again.

Before taking her paints out, she went upstairs and checked on her sons. Both were asleep, both faces of untroubled innocence. Sleep can do that, she thought. Wipes the day clean.

In the livingroom she pulled the other armchair over. Her easel was all smashed up and this the best substitute though she had to paint sitting down and felt she'd lost her perspective. Since she'd seen him under the bridge, she'd wanted to paint the old man. He'd looked so lost, so empty, a gaunt, tattered tramp. She hadn't seen a tramp since childhood and then she'd thought it romantic, wandering the countryside, no ties, no responsibilities. The stiffness in her hand grew as she painted.

The door opened. She put her palette down. Time to make supper. He smiled, glanced at her painting. Not time to make supper.

"That supposed to be me?" Chilling, then with his voice rising to that scream. "That supposed to be me?" Her face slammed into wet canvas, hair tore from the back of her skull.

"Don't waste my painting," she begged.

"Don't waste your painting? Don't waste your painting?" He let her go, ran through the kitchen, ran back with the carving knife. She ducked as he slashed. The painting split, folded. She ran for the door.

He caught up with her at the gate. His weight knocked her down, his fist fastened in her hair. The knife glittered in his hand.

"I'll come back in," she gasped. "I'll come back in."

"Naw. You wanted to be out." Dragging her. "It's your night to be out." She stumbled to her feet, compelled, head twisted. "I think you should go out." Over the road, over the grass. Wet splashed up to her ankles. The grass was black and silver. The lake of water just black. Snarling and snapping, it swallowed her. Spat her out. Swallowed her, spat her out. She stopped struggling. Blackness filled her eyes, her ears.

The iron-hard hands left her shoulders. Footsteps faded, spongily, toward home. Coughing, spluttering, vomiting up water, weeds and mud, she dragged herself out. The grass was slippery. She sat a long time, too cold to shiver, blinking her one eye. Everything round her was light and dark. The moon, out from behind rain cloud, was full. A yellow eye, staring back. Words sounded in her head.

"Where's my dinner. Where's my fucking dinner!"

"What's your fucking game. You answer when I speak, you hear!"

"You think I should go. Fucking want rid of me, is that it!"

"This is all you're good for. Fucking love it, don't you."

"I'll teach you. Bitch! Make a fool of me? Die, why don't you. Die."

His face reformed, the staring eyes, the spittle frothing on his mouth. The screaming pitch of his voice. She let the words slide past her into the bright dark night. They made her want to cry and that was not a good idea. His anger swelled up if she cried. Sometimes she thought the anger would swell him so much he would explode in a red, bloody mess in front of her, pieces of flesh flying everywhere. So she kept her surface smooth, glassily calm so that the words glanced off and streamed away. She pulled reed from her hair. Caked mud was drying in it. Her feet were still in the water, clothes tight round her body. Stiffly, she got up and stumbled towards home.

She ran a bath, washed her hair in it. Blood oozed from her

throat onto the towel. From her hands, from her thighs. She hadn't realised how much he'd cut her. The wounds don't hurt, she thought. It's the way he talks to me. Words. There was a pile of them somewhere. But she couldn't remember what they were.

The phone rang. She ran downstairs to get it before he woke.

"Hello?" Surely it was midnight.

"Mrs Bryson? Is that you?" The voice was female, unfamiliar, soft.

"Yes." Who else? There was a murmur of voices on the other end.

"Mrs Bryson, I just wanted to check if you were all right. Please don't hang up. I have your husband here."

"Where?" She looked in the bedroom. The bed was empty.

"The Samaritans. Your husband came in. He was very distressed. Is very distressed. He thought - well, he thought you were hurt."

She stared at the empty bed. He really wasn't in it. Must have gone off in his car. She was trying to hold on to that idea and what she could do with it when the woman spoke again.

"He says he damaged your painting. It - it made him angry."

Cradling the phone, she limped into the mess of the livingroom, rescued the shredded painting from under the spilled palette, the squashed paint tubes. The starved, hollow face of the tramp looked at her from an empty, despairing eye. It was a picture of utter nothingness. It was the only feeling she'd had to paint with. Her arms felt suddenly heavy. Something she couldn't deal with was about to swamp her. Struggling to solve this phone-voice, one thing swam up, solid and clear.

"Tell him I'm going to hang up," she said. " Then I'm going to call the police."

"Mrs Bryson, you're feeling very angry right now. And very hurt. That's understandable. But I think you should talk to your husband. Give him a chance to explain. He loves you very much."

"He told you that?"

"Yes. He's quite distraught. He's been threatening to kill himself. Talk to him. Please."

She had, of course, heard wrongly.

"What did you say?"

"I think he might harm himself. He's really sorry."

She'd heard right. It was unbelievable. He's mad, she thought. This woman's mad. I'm mad. She began to laugh.

"Tell him to come home," she said and hung up. Then she laughed and laughed and laughed though her face ached with the movement of it. When she stopped laughing, she put the phone back on the hall table and unlocked the front door. Really it was so simple. She was a calm, methodical person. Totally in control at all times. He required that from her. No outbursts, no tears, no laughter. Whatever he wanted, she was a straight line. Smooth, capable. An arrow.

She found the carving knife on the floor where he must have dropped it. In the livingroom, she sat down in the dark, in the middle of the mess, rocking back and forth. Paint tubes oozed, sticky like blood on each pendulum swing. Between her spreadeagled thighs, the knife stabbed every forward tick in the floor. Through the quiet night her ears strained for the sound of his car.

"Come on home," she crooned. "Come on home."

VICES

She sayd she heard vices. No the Joan o Arc kind, bit in hur heid. Ah wance asked hur whit they sayd, these vices, an wha did she think they wur. Bit hur answer wisnae repeatable. Except in wan o them modern plays ur oan a back street coarner it nicht. Aw the same, ye kent she did hear vices because she sometimes answered thum, while ye wur there, while ye wur in the middle o talkin tae hur. She'd answer somebody wha wisnae you wi an answer that hud nuthin at aw tae dae wi the subject up fur discussion.

In the middle o the back green, talkin aboot whether the sun wid ur widnae oblige the day, she'd suddenly say somethin like 'The buses don't go that way.' An ye'd be stood there wonderin whit that hud tae dae wi the price o cheese. It felt peculiar even whin ye wur yaised tae it because hur een chainged jist afore she spoke, gittin lichter coloured while the pupils shrunk tae wee black doats.

Last week, fur instance. It wis gaunae rain. She says so, fightin wi an airmfu wet sheets.

"There's nae dryin left. Gie it hauf an oor."

Ah sayd aye bit wurn't the gairdens needin it. Wid fairly bring the weeds oan.

"If you're going to keep on about it," she says. "The answer is

forty six." That wis anither queer thing. Whin she answered
wan o them vices she wis ayewis deid polite, correct like.

She hud a black ee, a richt shiner.

"Wis he it ye again?" Ah asked.

"Your turn," she says. "What's the square root of six thousand,
two hundred and forty one?" Noo, ah read an awfy loat o books
bit ah widnae ken a square root fae a club fit an sayd so.

"Aye," she says. "These'll dae better oan the pulley." An she
goes awa inside, a wee burd o a wummin trauchled aboot wi
slappin wet sheets that very nearly trip hur up.

Last nicht he wis shoutin again. Jist in the door an startit. Sam
an me wur sittin doon tae oor tea.

"Ah'm gaun roon there," says I. "He's at it again."

Sam stauns up.

"Ah'll go," he says. Noo, ma Sam's aw richt. Six fit three an
could chap sticks wi his bare hauns nae bother. Bit he'll take a
wee burd oot the cat's mooth an lit it go. Greets in a buckit
whin there's a sloppy film oan TV. The richt kinna man Sam is
an ah wisnae littin him git in bother fur a wee nyaff that widnae
keek in his back poakit.

"You sit tae yer dinner," ah says. "Ah'll go."

Somethin smashes tae pieces is ah hop the fence atween the
front paths. Bit whin he comes tae the door his face is aw nicey-
nicey an plaistered wi a luk o obligin enquiry.

"Kin ah help ye, Mrs McGreegur?"

"Ye kin help me aw richt," says I. "Ye kin help me an ma Sam
tae enjoy oor dinnur by lettin us huv it in peace, so ye kin. An
ah'd like a wurd wi yer wife if ye'll jist tell hur it's me."

Bit he's quick.

"Sorry aboot the noise," he says. "Ma dinnur plate wis hoat an
ah drapt it. Bit Netta's no feelin weel. She's huvin a lie doon.
Ah'll tell hur ye wur here." Then he shuts the door, richt in ma
face. Ah bang oan the knoaker again. This time his face isnae
sae obligin.

"Ah'm no budgin till ah speak tae Netta," says I. "An if ye shut the door again ah'll git the polis tae come aboot the disturbance."

He luks at me. His wee piggy een huv goat chips o blue in thum. Oh, ah'm annoyin him aw richt but he's no waantin the polis at his door eethur. He turns his heid and shouts ben the hoose.

"It's Mrs McGreegur waantin tae ken ye're aw richt."

"Ah'm fine." Hur vice comes back, thin is a reed. Then, "It was Lazarus who climbed the tree." Her man's mooth twists doon at wan coarner an he pushes his face intae mine.

"Ye see," he sneers. "Normal is ever." Ah manage tae resist the temptation tae shuv the sneer doon his throat an go back hame. Ma dinnur tastes like cauld saun.

"It's him that's daft," ah say. Bit somethin isnae richt. Och, ah ken he's thumped hur. He's ayewis thumpin hur an it's quate enough next door noo. Bit somethin isnae richt. "It's they bloody vices," ah say. "If hur heid wisnae fu o them she'd mibbe git hur wits thegither enough as git oot." Sam gies ma haun a quick squeeze. He's aw richt, ma Sam. He's gittin ready tae go roon the road tae the Scout hut.

"Gordon hud his dinnur?" He asks.

"It's in the oven," ah tell him. "Think he's keepin oot yer road." Sam jist noads. It's somethin atween faithur an son. Somethin fur them tae settle.

Oneywey, Sam goes aff roon the road an he's no awa five meenutes whin the rammy starts up again. No shoutin this time. Jist the kinna bumps an bangs ye'd raither no hear whin ye stey next a man like that. An because ah've goat ma nose in a book efter ma dinnur so it's real quate this side, ah kin hear his vice growlin atween thumps. No hurs though. She nivir makes a soond whin he's it hur. No a squeak.

So ah phone the polis. Ah've done it afore. They come, they go. Nuthin ever happens. This time we're roon aboot question number seventeen an ma patience is strung oot that ticht ye could play tap C oan it whin somethin bumps against ma front door. Ah dive ower tae open it an Netta faws in against me. She's a mess, bleedin, an a wee ruckle o bones in ma airms. So ah draw hur in, loack the door an sit hur doon oan the sofa. Ah dinnae ken whither tae greet ur sweer. Ah go back tae the phone.

"Oaficer," ah say. "That surmise you sayd ah wis surmisin jist fell in ma door hauf deid. Ah need tae phone an ambulence noo."

Ah don't mind the polis really. Ah don't mind o thum ever bein oan the spoat whin some pair sod's goat a knife it his throat. Bit jist lit a tail licht flick aff an thur there, savin the nation, puen ye ower.

Ah go back tae Netta afore ah phone the ambulence. She's a mess richt enough, burst lip, bleedin nose, baith een bruised. There's a big purple graze oan hur leg an she's sittin there, shudderin wi heaves too big fur hur wee thin frame tae contain, too faur gaun tae greet. Ah'm cleanin hur face whin the *open up, it's the polis* knock comes tae the door.

Twa fur the price o wan, as usual. Wan wi the questions an wan wi the een everywhaur, silent an supposed tae be intimidatin. Gie thum thur due, the wan wha's turn it is tae talk checks Netta ower richt awa. Pulse, quick luk it hur face, the state o hur, takin it aw in.

"Ambulence comin?" Ah noad. He gits hur name an address fae me then he squats doon oan his hunkers in front o hur an asks wan question.

"Kin ye tell me wha did this?"

Netta cannae speak. Then she coafs an mair blood trickles oot hur mooth.

"Wait for the bell," she says. The polisman luks it me, pintedly. He's bin here afore. Impittince is gaunnae choke me.

"Come oan, you ken wha did it," ah say. He shakes his heid.

"She's goat tae tell me." Then, "Unless you're a witness?"

Ma mooth opens tae gie him whit he needs. An ah tell him bit, even as ah'm tellin it, ah ken it's waistit braith. Whit dae ah ken. A black ee she nivir telt me aboot. Noises an shouts fae next door. Nuthin, that's whit ah ken. Nuthin.

The ambulence arrives then, lichts flashin, feet hurryin. Everythin buzzes it wance. They git Netta oan a streechur. Hur heid's limp noo, rollin aboot. Then, jist is they're gaun oot the door, *he* appears. The pitchur o innocence, aw concern.

"Ah seen the ambulence. Is awthing -" He comes tae an orchistratit stoap. Weel, disn't he suddenly recognise it's his ain wife oan the streechur. "Netta!" He gasps is the battered bundle is whisked aff doon the path. "Whit happened, whit - ?"

The polisman gits atween me an him is ah snarl somethin no quite foul enough tae describe whit he's up tae. Bit ah hear him.

"She went oot fur a walk, oaficer." Haltingly. "She hud a sair heid. Ah wis wunderin it hur bein sae long." Haud me doon, haud me back. The ambulence takes aff wi pair Netta oan hur ain, smashed up an helpless wi naebody tae sit worryin ower hur cause the yin that should is busy savin his ain lyin skin an ah'm walkin holes in ma carpet, spittin oot wurds ah nivir kent ah could say richt till this meenut.

If she hud been oot fur a walk this'd be the crime o the village, heidlines in the local paper: *Brutal Assault - chief constable vows to catch thug responsible.* Huh, ah could spit. Wunder if yon fitba player fancies the baseba bat in his face month efter month, year in year oot. Wunner hoo long it'd take afore his brain turnt tae mush!

Oor Gordon slinks in the back door in the middle o this an catches some o the flak. He's aw richt though, oor Gordon. Fifteen an nearly is big is his dad. Jist like him, is weel. Kens ah'm only lettin the pressure aff. Ah tell him the remain's o his dinnur's in the oven if he waants tae gie it a decent burial.

"Ah'm no hungry, Mam. Ah'll fix masell somethin efter." He

goes by me, up the stair. The backsides hingin oot his jeans an ah'm aboot tae tell him he kin fix that an all whin it hits me. That awfy familiar rip ah huvnae seen fur years.

"Zacchaeus," ah say. He stoaps mid-stair and turns roon. His face is awfy white. "It wis Zacchaeus that climbed the tree." His face crumples.

"Ah seen it, Mam. Ah couldnae git doon the tree. He wis bashin hur heid aff the waw. An layin intae hur. Wi his fists. An his feet."

He's greetin an ah'm haudin him, shushin him like ah yaised tae whin he wis wee. Whin he's quaeter, ah start tae ask him whit he wis daen up the tree bit ah ken the answer. It's a guid place tae hide an ye kin see in the windae an ken whin yer Dad's awa tae the Scouts withoot ye. Easier tae hide than say *Dad, ah dinnae waant tae go oneymair*. Bit Netta must hae seen him. The white face in the daurk branches. An she telt me. In hur ain queer wey, she hud telt me. Askin fur help.

"Ye huv tae tell yer Dad, son," ah say. "He'll lit ye be yer ain man. Bit you huv tae fund the courage tae say it." Ah send him tae waash his face. Then ah go next door.

He answers ma knoak. He's stull weerin his falseface, aw concern an peetyfu. Ah dinnae feel like hittin him oneymair. Jist contemptuous. Ah tell him it's the polis ah waant an the wan wha isnae talkin the day comes tae the door.

"See whin yer feenished takin doon the fairy story," ah say. "Ma son hus somethin tae tell ye."

Ah go tae the hoaspital efter. Netta luks better, nae blood. An worse, hur face purple, black an yella, missshaped wi wan ee a swollen, slantit slit. She haurly makes a bump in the bed. No the pickin o a sparra oan hur. An she's awa. Listenin tae vices in hur heid. Noo an again, answerin thum. Efter a while ah git up an go luk fur the doctur. He's young, fresh faced an serious.

"Skull fracture, broken ribs, bruises, cuts and abrasions. It's bad. But it'll heal." He kens aboot the vices, hus jist filled oot details fur a psychiatric examination oan a caird he's haudin. "In a week or so," he says. Then he luks as if he's puzzled. "I know her," he says. "She was my teacher in High School. Maths. Then she got married. Had a lot of absences after that and one time, well, she just didn't come back." He smiles, kinna sheepish-like, an manages tae luk aboot the same age as oor Gordon. "I think she's talking to her students," he says.

Ah go back tae say cheerio tae Netta, the teechur wha mairrit a lorry driver an goat loast. Ah waant hur tae ken she's safe noo, that she kin be whit she waants tae be instead o whit he makes o hur wi his fists an his tongue. Ah'm thinkin that she held oantae somethin that wis hurs wi they vices. That they ootwittit him in the end whin she lit me ken oor Gordon wis in the tree. Ah'm thinkin aboot Lazarus wha wisnae in the tree. Wha came back fae the deid.

Ah lean ower the bed. She's lukin straught it me.

"You really will have to work harder," she says. An the pupil o hur wan visible ee is a big black hole ah'm fawin intae.

THE EXCHANGE

Listen to me, Sally.

Naw. Ye're no bein nice. Go awa. Ah dinnae waant tae listen.

Sally. Sally? I want to talk to you.

Ah cannae hear. Ah've goat ma fingurs in ma ears.

You can hear me. I'll groan and scream and shout.

Naw, naw. Da'll come up. He'll say ah'm bein bad an ah'm no. Ah'll tell him it's you.

He won't believe you. I'll be very quiet and just smile. Then he'll tell you off again. You don't like it when he tells you off.

He wid so believe mi. He loves mi. He disnae love you. He says ah'm no tae talk tae ye.

He did not!

That's whit he meant.

He meant we shouldn't stand and chatter in the corner with all those people there. Just cause they couldn't hear what we were saying. That's why they bothered. Nosy things.

Wis nut. Wis because ae Mam. Ye're no supposed tae talk in a room wi a deid persin in it.

She couldn't hear. She can't do anything anymore.

Ah wish she wis stull here.

Silly Sally. Likes to be smacked? Likes to get her own tea and stay in her room. Doesn't mind being poor little Sally when

Mummy falls over at Parent's Day and has to be fetched home in Mr Dickson's car?

She wisnae weel. She wis no weel. Ah'm no listnin tae you oney mair.

She was drunk. She smelled just like the pub down the street. Everyone knows that.

Da sayd she wis seek.

Well, he told the minister she bought her sickness in a bottle. You heard him. He hated her too.

He gret it the funerul.

Grown-ups are supposed to cry at funerals. We didn't cry did we, Sally?

You widnae lit mi. Ah waantit tae greet bit you widnae lit mi.

Shh! I can hear them downstairs. Daddy and Grandma - there, they've gone now. Why does she have to be here?

Tae help Da luk efter the hoose. He hus tae wurk, ye ken.

We can manage by ourselves. We don't need her.

Ye bettur be guid whin she's here. Ur she'll pit stickin plaistur ower yer mooth an mak ye sit in yer room fur hoors readin the Bible tae mak ye guid. Like she done tae me last year whin Mam wis in the hoaspitul.

She won't do that to me. I can make her go away.

Stoap it! Ah'm no listnin tae ye oneymair.

Yes you are. Sally?

Ah'll no listen. If you say oneythin else ah'll tell oan ye. Ah'll tell thum ye'll no be quate an ye say wickit, wickit things.

Then I'll tell what we did to Mummy.

Ah didnae dae oneythin.

Sally doesn't remember. Sally doesn't remember.

Aye, ah dae. She wis lyin oan the bathroom flair. She wis stull seek.

She was snoring! Lying on the floor with her untidy clothes and her hair all messy and an empty bottle beside her. Snoring! She couldn't even say sorry for what happened at school. Sorry everyone laughs at you. Sorry, sorry, sorry. Bet she's sorry now though - oh, Sally remembers now. Remember how we took Daddy's special razor down. Click, click. Now it looks just like a butter knife. Mind out, it's sharp. It was Granpa's. Remember?

Ah ken that. Bit ah nivir touched it. Da sayd ah wis nivir tae touch it an ah nivir did.

Just like she always said she'd do it. It was easy. She didn't even move. And the handle got all slippy and it fell on the floor.

Naw, it wisnae like that. It wisnae! She wis oan the flair an ah went awa an whin ah come back she wis like that. Ah goat blood oan ma froak an Mrs Cambull come fae nixt door. She's killt hursell, she sayd. Finully went an done it. That's whit she sayd!

That's what they all said. Just like we knew they would.

Ah'm gaunae tell thum. Ah'm gaunae tell thum you did it. It wis you.

They won't believe you. Crazy child, they'll say. Why, they hardly know I'm here. Poor Sally, they'll say. She's not quite right. Always talking to herself. Lonely wee thing, always on her own. Sits and talks to herself for hours. Never make out a word of it, just mumbles. Poor thing. See - they hardly know I'm here.

Ah'm no alane. Ah'm no, ah'm no!

I know, Sally. You've got me. I'm your best friend.

Och wheesht, wheesht. There's Granny comin up the stair. She'll bring the stickin plaistur. Ye huv tae go awa noo.

Oh No. Sally has to go away. Don't be frightened. I can take care of Grandma.

LION RAMPANT

At Larbert Cross, the red lion groaned and drew his stone head further down onto his chest. He let his eyelids drop against the dull ache behind them. At his back the noise from the pub grew louder with merriment. The accordion danced out its rousing music and the fiddle screeched into the darkness threading its tune through the lion's ears. For the standard of the nation it was all too much. He turned his head and looked across the road at the lights of the Wheatsheaf.

No raucous music spilled from that open doorway, only welcome warmth and the hum of gentlemen's conversation. No clack of wooden clogs on sawdust scattered stone. Just the quiet turn of a card and the clink of glass. They used crystal glassware in the Wheatsheaf and bleached-white linen cloths, not foaming tankards of ale to thud down on bare wooden table tops to the cry of *Fill er up, fill er up!* The lion sighed.

Behind him the scream of the fiddle had stopped. The doors of the pub burst open and Jake the fiddler stumbled out, fiddle in one hand, Fat Nancy grasped by the other.

"C'mon lass," Jake said. "Nowt for nowt. Is'll play as good a tune wi'oot me fiddle, thee'll see."

He pulled Nancy close into the shadow of the building, she still supping from a tankard that dribbled foam down her chin.

The lion caught a glimpse of red calico, black stocking, white calf, white knee, white thigh. The fiddle lay propped, abandoned, against the corner.

From down the road sounded the soft thud of hooves on dirt. An elegant grey, plumed and tasselled, drew up a carriage to the doors of the Wheatsheaf. The driver, in tails and livery, stepped down and tapped once on the open doors.

"We should set the clocks by thee, Ben," the Squire said, coming out from the warmth of the hallway. "Be that road thick wi snaw or bogged wi mire, thee's never late." He heaved himself into the carriage, settled himself comfortable and leaned over for a last word with Duncan Masters, landlord of the Wheatsheaf.

"Ah'll have ma note back frae his Lordship next week, Masters. Tell him I says so an see if I don't. G'night to ye."

With a click from the driver's tongue the grey picked up dainty hooves and the carriage drove off into the night. But for the grunts of Jake and Nancy's moans behind him, the lion was alone again. He gazed up at the painted sheaf of corn on the sign opposite. Its yellow was the dried grass of the veldt and the heat of his homeland, the tawny shade of a mate and the sleep of a lion after the kill.

There was a rustle of skirt and the clink of coin and Nancy staggered back into the pub. There would be more business for her that night and the lion privy to it all. Inside the pub the accordion sang on and on, the feet stamped, voices roared in song, in challenge, in mirth. Would there ever be a night of quiet with just the gentle wash of sound like waves on a lake.

Jake re-possessed his fiddle, carried it over and set it down against the lion's rump while he fumbled with thickened fingers to do up his buttons. The lion's upper lip twitched and curled back, the fiddle an irritation on his haunch.

Jake coughed, hacked and spit. The gob of spittle dropped onto the lion's red paw. He flickered his eyes to narrow slits.

Now the man raked in his pockets. A pipe was knocked empty on the lion's heavy shoulder. Ash spilled down his frozen mane. Another fumbled search and the click of a tinder box. Held close to the lion's ear, the flint was struck on his brow and the tinder caught. It was too much. Too, too much for the sovereign beast.

Stiffly, ignoring the creak of his set joints, the lion lowered himself on all fours and padded over the road towards the Wheatsheaf Inn. Behind him was the soft thud as pipe hit stone, the zing of fiddle as it fell into empty space. And silence from Jake's round empty mouth till the flare of tinder singed his fingers and was blown out on a curse.

This was better. The lion picked a spot facing the crossroads where he could watch the world pass, let the din from the Red Lion fade to become background and filled his ears with the soft wash of talk. He settled down. Peace.

It was not to be. Jake, in ale-inspired amazement, gathered up pipe and fiddle and followed the lion.

"Hey," he said. "Thee canna dae that. Thee canna jist walk ower here an sit ye doon. Awa an git back whaur ye belang."

With shuttered eyes, the lion turned his head and looked at the man.

"Aye, ye maun look," Jake said. "See here, yon's the Red Lion ower there an you be a lion whit's red. Ye canna bide here." He tapped insistence of every word on the lion's shoulder. The lion curled his lip back. Red teeth bared, gleaming in reflected light.

"Ha," Jake laughed. "Ah'm no feart fae yer stane teeth." He put his face down to the lion's. Bulbous dripping nose to the hard drawn up nose. Soft flesh shoulder to the stone strength of the lion. And he pushed.

The lion was on his feet. Cold stone teeth closed through Jake's soft warm throat. And Jake was gone. Piece by piece. Antelope, zebra, man. It was all the same to the lion. Gulped intestine, torn flesh, crunched bone. None of Jake remained save his forgotten fiddle. The lion roared his kill, his pride, his majesty. He uttered that one night-shaking roar then he settled himself forever.

The sound drew Duncan Masters to the door of his Inn. He looked first towards the noisome gaiety of the Red Lion Hotel and then to the red lion, now recumbent by his own cornerstone. He walked up to the lion.

"Had enough o yon company, has thee?" He asked. A shriek of laughter from over the road split the air, the sound of tables clattered as yet another fight began. Masters shook his head.

"Canna say as ah blame ye, lion," he said. He ran a soothing hand under the lion's chin. It touched sticky warmth. In the light he saw his palm shining red. He stepped back. The fiddle sang out objection to his kick. Stooping he picked it up, turning it over in his hands.

" Aye, ye best bide here then," he said. " An say nowt. They'll be nane as can shift thee now, ah daursay." He crossed the road, propped the fiddle against the corner of the Red Lion Hotel and returned to his own establishment.

Once indoors he went down to his cellar and took up a can of paint left over from his sign. It was yellow as the dried grass of Africa, tawny as a lion in his prime. He handed pot and brush to the barrel boy.

"Away on upstairs, laddie," he said. "An paint yon bloody lion."

WILD FIRE

It was wildfire. There in the nodding heads, the knowing looks, the drone of mouths. Bees buzzing in a byke were not so loud. Trees howling at the wind made less sound. The village burned. Tongues licked the flames, each word a breath blown on the embers to keep it burning.

It was Annie-from-the-paper-shop. The tongue-wagger of weeks. With child. A bastard child by a Baxter lad. And her still walking the streets. Shameless. Hadn't they known she'd come to a bad end. Didn't they remember saying so many a time when she walked by. Her with those plump full breasts and swinging hips, her painted nails and her painted eyes and her painted lips. A trollop she was, and they knowing it. A tart. Hindsight was making prophets of them all.

The prophets of the pit, on the other hand, made do with boasting of what she'd missed. And they swore of chances gone when the gleam in her eye and her ready smile had favoured them. The black burrows of coal sighed for her eager arms and her young skin until the lad himself, Bert Baxter, fell among them and stopped their dreaming. Now, sometimes, they toasted him man among men and other times, in envy, they roasted him.

"See what you get for your sins," they said. "Sent down here to scratch in the bowels of hell."

"Along with the rest of you," Bert threw back. But his hand shook all the same. His father, a pitman, had got a place for his son when it became clear he'd have to get wed. Shut away under ground, sweat black on his black vest, the rumble of coal trucks loud down the line, Bert laboured.

Jack Douglas saw the boy shit scared of the dark, of the heat and the tons of soil weighted, preposterous on the pit props, above them. A thin beam of light scanned the roof with each turn.

"Putting the evil eye on it, laddie?" He asked. "Watch long enough and you'll see what you're looking for."

Jack swung his pick. They were on piece work and it irritated to be slowed for a slip of a lad. Beside him Archie, his mate, worked steadily. They were a good team. Ton a week better than any other. The boy had better load faster or they'd bury themselves. Or him.

Light flickered again on the nearest upright. Jack threw down his pick.

"Come here." He grabbed at Bert's arm. It was soft, more limp than a woman's. He pulled the lad close to the prop, let go and put both hands on the wooden shaft.

"See. It'll no shift." He grunted, putting his weight into shaking it. "Solid as a rock that is. You try. I'd put a pound on you'd no even raise some stoor."

"Let the lad be," Archie butted in. "He'll come right."

Jack took up his pick again.

"Aye, Well, we know that," he muttered. "Wouldn't think he had it in him." And he swung as if to tear the bowels from the earth. Archie wiped a river of sweat from his neck with the tail of his vest.

"Jees, it's a hot one the day." Behind them, coal clanged into the truck.

"Comes of getting too near hell-fire," Jack grunted.

When the shift was done they filed into the cage and wound up to the surface. Already it was day, the blood-red stain on the sky turning blue. Blind as moles, they trudged to the rattle of chain past incoming workers. The day-shift all ready for search and drop. The pit never slept.

Sleep left Jack quickly when he woke, never lingered yawning on him as it did on some. He ate by the fire, in his socks. The table was for family meals. Shoes were for outside.

"Fancy, our Lizbeth, thirteen," Martha said, moving birthday cards aside. "Teenagers they call them, like they were a new breed." She had put on her coat and stood at the sideboard, getting ready.

"Be working before we know it," he said.

"Well, I hope she'll stay on at school. She's clever. She should get the chance."

Jack put his plate down on the hearth and took up his mug of tea. Often, he couldn't tell what Martha was thinking. He didn't like that, as if she did it to annoy him. Then she would speak, like now, when she should have nothing to say. So he ignored it. That way she let him alone.

"Where are you off to anyhow?"

"Annie's house. Said I'd give a hand to scrub out for she's not fit. Seventeen. Not much of a start, is it?"

"They'll know how it got there. I'd've used the shotgun on him if she'd been mine."

He watched his wife go then he filled out more tea. The dryness of the dust was always in his throat and he had a thirst for tea that was legendary. Fresher now from food and drink, he felt temper freshen with it. Martha should be in her own house not scrubbing some other man's floor. Man! That one'd never make a face worker. Let it get to him. Thought about it all the time. Does no good to think about it. Just do the job and get out. Did a job on Annie-from-the-paper-shop all right, though.

The metal gate sounded and feet came round the path. He

listened as the door opened and shut. Lizbeth came through from the kitchen.

"You're early," he said. She stopped in the doorway.

"Got sent home. Sick. Where's Mum?"

He saw her hand tighten on the strap of her schoolbag. The heaviness of books in it weighed on her shoulder, pulling her blazer apart.

"You don't look sick. What's wrong with you?" He could see she was growing up. The slight swell of pre-pubescent breasts rose under her blouse as she sighed. She had that look on her face again, shutting him out. God damn it, he was trying to get along with her. Her hand reached for the hall door, opening it as she spoke.

"Is Mum upstairs?" She shouted, "Mum?"

"She's not in." The schoolbag was still on her shoulder. She could put it down, at least. Have a cup of tea with him instead of hovering in the doorway. "You going to bed or making a draught?"

Lizbeth shut the door.

"Well, where is she?"

"Out, I tell you." There was no call for her to be running over to Annie's. He didn't want her round there, getting ideas. Least of all when Bert was about. No telling who he'd get round to trying next, seeing how he liked them young. And Lizbeth - Lizbeth was just ripe for it.

"Come on over by the fire."

She didn't move. Was trying to think where her mother would be, he knew. Made him angry that, like he wasn't good enough. Like she wanted to run. Like she was afraid of him.

"I'll see if you've a temperature."

"I haven't."

"Let me be the judge of that." Out of his chair, he caught her arm as she stepped away and pulled her nearer the fire. He pressed a rough palm on her brow. The slow swirl in his gut wanted his hands on her.

"I haven't. Miss Wotherspoon took it."

Her forehead was cool though beads sweated on her lip. Her chest heaved and those small breasts moved under the cotton cloth. If it wasn't Bert Baxter, there'd be some spotty lad wanting his hand in there to touch those swelling nipples. Some boy's hand on her bare white thigh, touching her, wanting her.

He felt his own sex grow stiff and hard, begging for touch and the warm wet yield of flesh. He'd have the arms and legs off any boy that laid hands on his Lizbeth. She was his, his.

"I'll see if Mum's at the shop." She turned, tried to jerk free but his grip on her arm brought her back round. The bag crashed to the floor.

"You're too big to go running for your Mum every five minutes."

The words pushed past the thickness in his throat. Now, on his knees, he pressed his face into those growing breasts, still holding tight to her arm. The familiar stiffness was about her as he felt the back of her knee, the warmth of her thighs, the curve of her buttocks.

"Dad."

He saw her hands clenched in fists at her sides. How could she mind when he needed her. Fingers trembling, he touched the fine down of hair, searched the changes in her. She was all grown up, dry and tight, but ready. And she was his.

His weight brought her down onto the rug, her voice a whimper in his dinning ears. He struggled, one-handed, with the fastening on his trousers. A patter of blows rained on his hot head and burly shoulders.

"No, Dad. Don't. I'll do anything you say, anything. Don't do that to me. Please."

Her words cut him up inside. He was bursting out of his clothes, burning with need. She shouldn't want him left like this.

"Anything I say, Liz. When it's you blocks the bedroom door." She wouldn't shut another door against him in his own house. Not now. She'd see. Wasn't anything - to be afraid of. He didn't look at her face as he thrust into her, felt her close round him. She had stopped struggling.

He was driven now, all crazed up, desperate for release. He jerked her hard up against him and was spent in her. When it was gone he edged away, crawling backwards on his knees, not looking at how she lay. He got himself, covered, back into his chair, wrung out. He couldn't look at her lying there on the rug. A broken thing. Wounded and wasted. The firelight bit into his eyes, stung them.

"You best get on up to bed." His voice was rough, jagging in his throat.

It was a long dead minute till she moved, covered herself and got, unsteady, to her feet. He stared into the fire, trying not to hear the sound as her walking dragged over to the hall door. When it was shut behind her and her limping feet trailed to silence on the stair, he put his head in his hands and wept.

Gulps of air gasped in at his mouth and wheezed out of him. Breaking like a tidal pain, sobs wracked his body. He did not know why he cried. His chest heaved fitfully, his rough hand rubbed across his eyes.

It was a fool would cry for a thing done. Surely, he had never meant to. When Martha came home, he would tell her. She'd know what to do. He heard his voice say the words and felt better. He imagined her face and it held loathing. He was cursed. Condemned he would be, from his own mouth. No, he could not tell Martha.

He bent over, stirred the fire back to life with the poker and sat staring at the red coal. When he heard his wife's feet come round the path he lifted his paper, opened it and sat back in his seat.

The schoolbag in the middle of the floor prompted Martha as

soon as she saw it.

"She's sick," he said, knowing the words would take her straight upstairs where she musn't go. Not yet. Fear weakened his wits as she turned for the hall door. He hated her for this fear, for making him scrabble around for the right words.

"I've just been up," he cleared his throat. "She's sleeping." He wanted to scream at her as she stood there, hand glued to the door knob. Get into the fucking kitchen where you should be. This is my business. I break my back to keep her. His hand shook with the effort of controlling the anger.

"Let her be," he said. "She'll want fed when she wakes up." He rustled the newspaper, stared at the black print and waited to be swept away by tongues, torment, voices. Lizbeth would tell. Make a big thing of it. Make him look the wrong one when it was her. Asking for it.

Martha turned away from the door, unfastening her coat.

"I'll see how she is after dinner," she said.

With her safe in the kitchen, Jack sat further into his chair. A couple of hours. It'd be all right in a couple of hours. Not given to hysterics was Lizbeth. Like enough, she'd be sleeping already. The newspaper began to grip his attention. Bad news. Always it was bad news. He wondered if they just didn't look for the good. All was right with his world. His wife in the kitchen, daughter asleep upstairs. He stretched out his shoeless feet and relaxed.

SMAW COARNER

This is ma piece o paper. Ah'm gaun tae write oan it, ma piece o paper. This time ah'll pick up an implement an make marks oan somethin white an untouched an virginal. Ah dinnae like that wurd. Virginal. Dinnae ken whey bit ah dinnae like it. Ah'm no. Wisnae oneywey. Virginal, that is. Bit somethin wis. Funny that, ah ken somethin hus bin touched that wis nivir touched afore. Somethin's broken. Somethin that cannae be mended, that ah didnae even ken wis there, is broken noo an cannae be fixed. An ah didnae even ken ah hud it. Funny that. Ah didnae ken aboot it, stull cannae pit a name tae it, only ken it's real cause it's no there. Hurts like hell.

Aye, it dis. Ah kin feel that. Like liquid fire in the middle o me. The kinna hurt ye'd like tae dig yer hauns intae an rip oot. The kinna hurt that makes me waant tae rip ma boady tae bits. If ah could grab haud o ma ankles an jist rip me in twa, then fower, then aicht. Like a bit o paper afore gaun in the bin. Like this bit o paper. Like ah could rip me up. Only ah cannae. Ah cannae cause it isnae possible tae actually physically dae it. The next best thing, the next best thing is whit ah dun wi the razor.

See yon nurse. See the wan that sayd *Ye're a silly lassie. They marks wullnae go awa. Ye'll ay huv scars.* She thinks ah'm daft. Ah think she's daft. Ah'm lyin here, hurtin in the middle. Hurtin wi a big, roon, rid, burnin kinna hurt that wullnae ever stoap and she's tellin me ah'll huv scars. Ah could laugh. Ah could laugh bit ah'd only greet an then ah'd no be able tae stoap an ah'm no gaun tae start oneything ah cannae stoap. Mibbe ah better stoap stickin this pensul in ma airm or they'll come an tak that awa an all.

Ma airm. Ken, ye luk it yer airm an ye hate huvin an airm. Hate huvin tae say ma airm. Cause if ye've goat an airm ye've goat ither bits. An aw they bits make a boax. An aw that's in the boax is a big, jaggin, hoat, hurtin an ye cannae git in the boax tae git it oot. An whin ye try they stoap ye.

See that doctur. He's tryin. An ah dinnae waant him tae git in ma boax cause he disnae waant tae git it oot. No like ah wid git it oot, if they'd let me, if it could be done.. He jist waants tae tak a look, that's aw. Jist waants tae tak a fuckin look, that's aw. Like ah'm an object fur sale. Like this is the antiques road show an he'll jist check me oot fur clues is tae where an when an hoo an whit am ah wurth oneywey. So he talks an ah luk it the flair. An sumtimes he disnae talk an ah luk it the flair. Ah'm no gaun tae luk it him. Ah dinnae waant tae see his een lukin it me, seein me. Or seein oneything inside me. He gits fed up an then they bring me back.

Weel, if he kent sae much he'd ken withoot me helpin that is husnae goat wurds. If ah could puke it up, if ah could actually puke it up he could huv a guid luk it it. He could poke it aboot, stir it roon, stick it unner a fuckin microscope if he waantit tae. Be aw right that wid. Then it widdnae maitter if he kent fur ah'd be rid o it an widdnae need him or hur or the rest o thum wi they're quate squeakin feet an pattin o pillaws an takin ma temperature an feedin me pills, pills an pills. If ah could git it oot they widdnae be seein me at aw, wid they? Whey don't they ken that much, it least.

Even ma mum. Ah should be sorry she's worrit. Ah think ah should be bit ah luk it her een an the worries lyin roon thum an the sorry puzzles lyin in thum an ah cannae feel oneything except hoo ah wish she wid go awa so's she didnae huv tae sit there accusin me wi hur een o gien hur sumthin she cannae unnerstaun or explain tae awbody. So ah guess that bit o me's no workin noo. The bit that dis the luvin stuff. Mibbe that's whit goat broken.

Ah dinnae ken. Ah dinnae waant tae ken. Ah dinnae waant tae think aboot it. An they aw waant tae make me think aboot it. An talk aboot it. An huv it aw jump aboot jaggin, an punchin, an kickin, an bitin, an screamin in ma heid again. Naw.

Naw, ah'll jist keep it whaur it is. Hurts like hell bit it least ah dinnae huv tae luk it it. They cannae make me luk it it if ah dinnae gie it names. That nurse cannae. She thinks ah'm daft. *Silly*, she says. Then, *Lucky*.

"Ye're lucky tae be here, ye ken."

Wha's daft? Cannae make up her mind, kin she.

An no ma mum. She jist sits there. Like a wee licht that's burnin an wishes it wisnae. She disnae touch me. Ever. She's a bit feart fae me noo. Like ah wis a mad dug that micht bite. Too feart tae touch me less ah dae sumthin else strange. Jist as weel. If she did, if she touched me, if she pit hur airms roon me, if she held me. Weel. Ah micht be in real trouble then.

PICTURES IN BLACK & WHITE

They had kept a picture. Her sitting on her father's knee, outside, on the garden seat beside the lawn. The sun was high and both faces had dark shadows under the eyes, under their chins. It must be the only picture of her in the house. She snatched it up and walked through to the livingroom where she threw it down on the coffee table.

"Why did you keep it?" She demanded. Her mother's lips tightened, but her eyes wore that *here we go again* look.

"It was the only one. You burnt all the others."

"I *meant* to burn them." She was screaming now, couldn't stop herself, and she didn't want to be screaming. "Why won't you understand. Why won't you ever understand?" Her mother stood up.

"He's your father." Tight-lipped. Dry. A statement of a fact.

"He's dead now." Why wouldn't her voice come back down from that awful caterwauling pitch. She forced herself to speak slowly. "Now we could have the truth. At least that."

They stared at each other, the young woman and the old one. Lindy wanted justice. Her hope of it swelled as her mother's eyes filled, then spilled away with her words.

"If you've come back to torment me, I think you should leave again. I can't take this, Lindy. I can't take this. Your father and me had a good life. A nice family." The words were still casting their spell as Lindy shut the door on it. She was half way down the street when she remembered she'd let the photograph lie on the table.

He was breathing in her ear. Hot, damp and heavily.
"Jason, don't."
"What d'you mean, don't?" He squeezed her breast, ran his thumb over her nipple.
"I mean don't. I don't want to."
"Och, you do." His mouth nuzzled her neck, his knee pushed between hers. "You know you do."
Afterwards she got up, made herself a cup of tea. Outside it wasn't quite dark. Grey houses, black chimneys, grey sky. The tea made a warm spot deep inside her. Why didn't *she* know if *he* knew.
She wandered back into their bedroom. He was asleep, one arm flung carelessly across her pillow, his head turned away. In the half light through the blinds the hollow where her head had been was black. Deeply indented. I'm still there, she thought. I haven't risen. I'm not standing here drinking a cup of tea and looking at my marriage bed as if it were a strange land. I am in it, and a shadow.
Rather than slide into her black skin, she took her tea into the kitchen and sat there, clutching the cold cup until morning coloured the sky.

The coffee machine hissed, its liquid note rising as the cup filled.
"We'll have to stop meeting like this." Roger Buchanan's fat fingers trailed up her spine. She ignored him, bent to raise the perspex cover and take her coffee. His fingers clamped round her arm, just beneath her armpit, stopping movement and blood.

"Allow me," he said, taking her cup and holding it out. He stared at her breasts, making her naked. "Anything for a lady," he suggested as his fingers loosened and, almost accidentally, the touch was intimate. Grotesquely intimate.

To get away from where he was, she took her coffee into the washroom. Sat the cup on the ledge and ran cold water over her shaking hands. Anger boiled inside her with no place to go. Karen sloped in, big bust, big hips, a round, honest face. She looked men straight in the eye.

"Why does he do that to me?" Lindy said. Karen pursed pink lips.

"That's why," she said. "You think there's a reason. Don't think. Grab his balls. Squeeze 'em hard. Don't think. He doesn't."

"Touch him!" Lindy shuddered. Karen was running water into a basin.

"No. Don't touch him. You'll only encourage him. Have him coming back for more." She shook water drops off flashing, multi-ringed fingers. "Hurt him," she said. "Hard." The towel rail clattered as she tugged it to a clean bit. "My first day, he sat on my desk, peered down my shirt. I said *Piss off, pal!* Loudly. So everybody could hear. D'you know what he did?"

"What did he do?"

"Jumped up smartish. *Christ, another fucking feminist*, he says. Never looked near me again. You've got rights, you know."

Lindy let out her breath in a long whoosh, shaking her head.

"I couldn't - all that legal stuff."

"Naw." Karen patted her hand. "The right to be you."

The door swung behind her leaving Lindy with cold coffee and the need to stare at her mirrored white shirt, black skirt reflection.

She was on the tube, strap hanging and struggling with french bread and salad shopping. An enormous tweed-suited woman filled the space at her armpit. A body pressed up against her back, a grey business suit stood, starched to her shopping. Every buckle of the carriage brought pressure from the knees of a lad in jeans seated in front of her. No-one looked at anyone else. A way of not consenting to territorial invasion, of being absent while present. What was she doing in a city? Running away from space?

Brakes grated, bodies leaned, the train stopped. Another press of people, shuffled, re-arranged. The train juddered, a name plate passed, the hypnotic left, right sway of the carriage and into the black tunnel, the concentrated glare of light. Skin on her thigh prickled. Stop it, she told herself. Enough is enough. The touch on her leg persisted, travelled round the curve of her backside. Not pressure. A caress.

"I am not a photograph," she said. Firmly. Aloud. Nobody moved. The boy in jeans looked up, briefly. The hand stayed.

She squinted round. Grey suit beside her, a glimpse of purple and orange mohawk behind. She tilted her head as far left as it would go.

"Excuse me," she said to the business suit. "Could you help with my shopping. It's falling." An inclined nod to the bag hanging at her knees. The hand moved.

"No. It's all right," she said ."I've got it now."

The brakes bit. In the forward sway she looked down, glimpsed grey shoe tucked tight against her black court. She lifted her heel, twisted her foot round. The brakes screamed. She put all her weight on that one, vicious spike. The business suit buckled, yelled. And yelled. The sway stopped, doors opened. She stared at the noise from the open mouth.

"Oh. Did I step on your foot," she said. And got off the train.

"You don't know," she said.

Jason had just come in. He stared at her.

"*I* know," she added. " I know what I want and when I want it."

"Yeh?" Helpfully. He hadn't taken his jacket off but stood, in the middle of the Indian carpet, beside the oatmeal lounger, staring at her as if waiting for the punch-line. She felt patient, calm.

"When I say I don't want sex, you always say I do."

"I don't." He grinned. It was a familiar grin. One she'd thought endearing. Ingenuous, it went with blue eyes and fair hair. She realised she'd said sex instead of love-making. Many a true word spoken, she thought. And at the same time knew she didn't want either. Not with him. Not any more. She'd stood too far back, for too long, to make contact now.

"I've packed," she said. "If you won't discuss this sensibly, I'm going to Karen's till I find a place of my own."

"You don't mean that," he said.

She left.

The village was cool green, latticed with trees, rooftops cut out of a wider sky.

"I wasn't expecting you," her mother said, as always looking right through her. This time at the neat, blossoming front rose garden. Lindy gathered her edges together.

"Mum," she said. "I love you. All I ever wanted was that you would love me. Enough to listen properly. To see me. He made me hide. But you rubbed me out with your *nice family* invention. I've had to invent myself."

Her mother looked at the whorled Axminster floor. She looked at the corniced ceiling, at the chintz sofa, at the pale blue velvet curtains. Her eyes filled with tears. Then she looked at Lindy. Lindy in a red sweater and blue jeans. Lindy, with corn coloured hair and hazel eyes. Solid. Truthful. Not needing justice any more.

"I know," her mother said. "I burnt that photograph."

Karen was twittery.

"Just give 'em a good squeeze," she said. " That'll bring a blush to his cheeks."

Lindy grimaced.

"I couldn't. Each to her own, huh?"

The coffee machine spluttered, the spurted note rising as the cup filled to the brim. Lindy bent over.

"What an invitation," Buchanan's voice sang out at her back, his hips pressed onto her buttocks. She straightened, took a step back into the confined space between filing cabinets and coffee machine. His bulk shadowed the rest of the office, shutting out light, people. She put her left hand on his chest.

"What invitation is that?" She smiled, running her fingers down the buttons of his shirt. He squirmed.

"You're doing terrible things to me," he whispered, moving close. She hooked her fingers into the waistband of his trousers, and pulled.

"Oh, I know," she said. And poured the coffee, black without sugar, down the V-shaped gap at his waist. The scream rose to white-hot pitch.

"Oh dear," she said. "Look what you've made me do."

WALKIN OAN WATTER

Like craws roon a coarpse, they ur. Yin wid come, yin wid go, the occaishunal steer roon. Wid tak the skil bell tae fricht thum, flytin awa, skirts flappin, back tae thur hames. They pairt tae lit me through like ah wis Moses it the Rid Sea. Pairt bodies an bletherin. Ye ken hoo quate it goes whin they've bin talkin aboot ye an they stoap. Ah walk by intae the shoap through that kinna quate. They're the same wummin, near enough, wha waitit ootside ma hoose three year afore whin Danny's boady wis brocht hame fae the pit. Then, neethur wantit nur needit, thur grey silent simpithy made the bile rise in ma throat. Noo, the same bittur taste comes back. Isa Cameron is haudin coort. Ah feel hur een borin intae ma back. Een like studs she's goat. Ah keep ma heid up an walk by. Widnae gie hur the satisfaction.

The noayse picks up is the door shuts ahint me. They'll move noo, somewhaur else. Meg hus Mr Thomson's papers ready.

"By, it's a grand day," she says.

The door opens again, the roar o a coal lorry it the curb droonin ma answer. Through coal stoor, Bert Baxter beams it the twa o us.

"If it wisnae Merch, it kid be summer," he says.

"You cannae be sae gled is the rest o us tae see an upturn in the weathur," ah tell him. He's done weel tae huv goat hissell oot the pit.

"Ach, it'll no last, bit," his grin widens.

"See ye're takin oan help." It wis congratulaishuns an he kens it, he's young tae be makin his ain wey, bit his face gits serious.

"Aye, an ah'm needin somebody tae help wi the books," he says. "Kin ah no steal ye awa fae the manse, Ella. Ye're the only wan ah ken kin coont abin ten an ah've nae heid fur figurin."

"Ye've done weel enough withoot coontin, then," says I.

"Bit ye'll think aboot it?" He says. Ah luft the meenisturs papers an go. The wurk it the manse suits me fur aw it's nae differint tae whit ah've done aw ma days. Twa year since the meenistur come new tae the place, a bachelur needin a hoosekeepur. Bein a widda won me the joab ower the heids o ithers wha thocht thursells mair fittin tae be daen fur an un-wed meenistur, safe is they wur fae waggin tongues bi thur mairridge beds.

Ah've nae patshince wi thur back-tae-front morality. Me, wi twa dochturs tae rear single-haundit an no a penny commin fae the pit bi wey o compensaishun. Nae faw it the face taen ma man. Wis his ain guid hert gied oot. Bit ah'm tryin tae lit the sun draw the sting oot thur talk though it burns in me aw the same Like a hoat coal. Aw the wey up tae the Manse an me tryin tae damp it doon. Taks the meenistur tae pit it oot. Ah'm in the back door an there he is, up oan a stool, cassock fleein aboot, pentin the kitchen bricht yella.

" Whit ae ye daen?"

"Sunshine," he says, near fawin aff the stool tae luk roon it me. "You sayd it wis dull in here. No enough light." He waves the brush, drapin pent oan his cassock. "Sunshine," he says. He's makin a helluva mess.

Ah tak ma coat aff.

"That'll nivir waash," ah say.

"It's done," says he, haudin up an airm. " Moths." There's a muckle great teer fae airmpit tae waist.

"Musta hud teeth an auld wummin'd kill fur." Isa Cameron, ah'm thinkin. As if hur tongue's no sherp enough.

"Ye'll no be misled, wull ye, Ella," he says. "Ah confess ah tore it climbin through that windae there efter loackin masell oot last Sunday. You, it is, wha keeps me organised." It's mair'n he's said tae me in twa year. Must be the spring hus brocht him oot his study an me wi a waashin tae dae, the cleanin tae start.

Taks us an hoor tae feenish the pentin then he's awa oot ma road, back tae his sermon. That's yaisially aw he talks tae me aboot. Whin he waants an opeenyin. Wance he asked whit ah thocht aboot the stoarm it Gallilee. Ah telt him walkin oan watter wid be easy compairt wi some. Divint we dae that withoot thinkin hauf the time. *Noo, there's an idea*, he sayd, an turnt back tae his papers wi barely a noad tae lit me ken ah kid go.

Ah roll up ma sleeves an fetch the heavy drapes doon fae the upstairs rooms. By eleevin they're blawin oan the rope, the kitchin's straucht an ah've his tea-tray ready. Ah chap it the door afore gaun in.

"Yer tea," ah say, gein him a meenut tae clear a space in the clutter oan his desk so's ah kin set it doon.

"You work too hard, Ella," he says, shufflin his papers oot the road.

"Ah dae whit needs daen," ah tell him. "An ah widnae mind in here tae turn it oot, whinever ye've a mind." He turns tae luk up it me.

"You should bring yer ain tea in here. Huv a seat."

"No," ah say, makin tae go.

"Wait." His vice stoaps me an ah sit doon. He'll be waantin tae read whit he's written. Ah think sometimes he jist likes tae try oot the soond.

Insteed o speakin, he shuffles his papers again, lukin it thum as if the wurds dinnae mak oney sense. The open bible an referince books lie scattert roon aboot the tray. Ah fauld ma hauns in ma lap an wait. There's silence. A froon creases his broo. He luks puzzled. Then he taps the spin oan the side o his cup.

"Ah think we should marry," he says. His vice soonds like it's cummin fae a lang wey back. Ah'm lukin it the croon o his heid. A shaft o sunlicht shows up the grey sprinklt in his hair. Ootside the drapes ur in ful sail. They'll be ready fur irenin afore ah go hame.

"Whit?" Ah say.

He luks it me noo. He's awfy pale, needin a touch o the sun. The set o his jaw disnae go wi the ascetic shut-in colour o him.

"I think we should marry," he says again. Jist that. Disnae gie oney reasin. Disnae add oneything. Jist that. An keeps his een haudin mine.

Ah luk doon it ma hauns. It ma fingurs, rough an rid wi the coanstint scoor o scrubbin an waashin. In thum is years o watter, hoat an cauld, slappin sheets an bittur winds, steamin heat fae coontless meals, the haunlin o a bairn's saftness luftit tae the breest, the touchin o a man's boady in pashin an grief.

"Ah think no," ah tell ma sair worn hauns. Eethur he ignores me ur he disnae hear.

"Ye can lit me know," he says. "In a day or so." He hesitaits, as if he micht add somethin, then he turns again tae his sermon, starin it it, stull lukin puzzled. Ah go back tae the kitchen. Feelin like ah'v bin asked if we should huv a new cairpit fur the lobby, ah wurk ma time oot. Whin ah feenish ah pit ma coat oan an shout ah'm awa is if nuthin differint hus passed atween us. Mairry him. The thocht cannae even cullect itsell tae be a thocht. Naw, ah huv maistered ma situashun whin wance ah thocht it wid maistur me. Noo ah'v nae wish tae chainge it.

"Man's aff his heid," ah tell the burn is ah pass ower the brig. "Mad is a Mairch hare."

The cluster o wimmin hus shiftit tae the coarnur ae

Quarrybrae Road, tongues stull flappin haurder than the sheets oan thur lines. Isa Cameron's haudin sway in thur middle, drippin wi pisen. She nurses a grudge fur huvin bin pit oot ma hoose the day Danny wis brocht hame. Hur it wis, daured entur ma hame an vice the opeenyin that a black burial in the heat an sweat o the pit wid huv made a better daith tae mourn.

Fur shame he's tae go that wey, she sayd. *Whin he couldae went unner the coal an left ye somethin tae git by oan.* She'd hae burrit a guid man alive tae pit breed in the mooths o ma bairns bit she'll no allow me the richt tae wurk fur it fae a man wi nae wife tae guerd him.

Nae doot it wis ma jaunt in the meenistur's caur last week that geid rise tae this roond o talk. He wantit ma help tae pick a new suit, insistit. An ah went kennin ah'd be seen galivantin, an be flingin fresh meat tae Isa Cameron. Ah gie a noad is ah pass by. Lit thum talk thersells intae tangles, ah'll hae nae truck wi thur blethers.

Wance inside, the hale day's gaun roon in ma heid. He shouldnae huv spoke. Ma situashun's made impoassible by it. Ah waantit nae chainge bit chainge there'll huv tae be. Whin the weans come hame, ma mind's made up. We sit doon tae dinnur an Linda pits the seal oan it.

"Ah met Bert Baxter doon the road," she says. "Ah'm tae mind ye whit he sayd this moarnin."

"He waants me tae dae his book-keepin fur him," ah tell hur.

"An gie up the manse," she says. "Wull ye dae it?" Jane luks up fae hur soup, watchin me.

"Ah wull," ah tell thum. Jane's face breks intae a smile.

"That'll soart Mrs Cameron," she craws. The meenut the wurds ur sayd, hur heid gaes doon again. Ah'm starin it hur.

"Whit hus ma wurk tae dae wi Isa Cameron?" Ah ask hur, kennin ma vice is cuttin hur like a knife an no bein able tae help it. Jane disnae answer, she's stoaped eatin, her heid's stull bent. "Ah wull ken," ah say, "whit Isa Cameron hus tae say aboot ma wurk."

The wean luks up it the ceilin. She's waantin help an ah'm no able tae gie hur oney.

"Jist that it wisnae richt - things - like that." An ah cannae lit it rest. That ma ain dochtur's bin held tae accoont tae that wummin's lashin tongue!

"Go oan." She luks it me wi tears in hur een.

"That ye wur in Mr Thomson's caur. She sayd ye'd huv mair sense -"

"Ye ken fine weel whit she's bin sayin," Linda bursts oot. "It's no Jane's faut!" Ah feel angur rise, hoat inside me. The luk in Jane's een telt me she hauf believed whit wis bein said. The day's tiredness faws aff me an ah git up.

"Time ah dealt wi Isa Cameron," ah say an mairch oot the door.

Afore ah kin turn fur the hoose ah'm wantin, ah see the wimmin staunin whaur ah passed thum oan ma wey hame. Ye'd think they hudnae moved. Bit ma dander's up, stridin me oan an ah wid face a hunner bletherin wimmin fur whit ah've tae say. They mean tae pit a telephone boax oan that coarnur. Weel, they'll need shift Isa Cameron apiece furst!

Martha Douglas sees me cummin. Martha ah coont is a freend an she opens hur mooth tae speak bit nae soond comes oot is ah stride by her richt intae the middle o thum.

"Ah'll huv a wurd wi you, Isa Cameron," ah say. She luks it me, gies a sniff.

"Oh aye."

"Aye! An the rest o ye kin jist hear me oot." Ah stoap the drift awa an plant masell square in front o the interferin auld bissum. "Fur years ah've stuid back an sayd nowt while ye've shuved yer nose intae ma business, Isa. Bit ah'll staun idle nae longer. Ye think tae throw enough durt an it'll stick. Well, think again, for ye'll not rub ma lassie's nose in durt o yer ain makin!" Ah huv tae draw braith an she's in there quick.

"Ha!" She snoarts. "There's nae smoke wi oot fire!"

"An some fowk licht thur ain fire," ah'm waggin ma fingur unner hur nose. "Aye, an fan the flames noo an again tae keep it burnin. Weel, ye're done wi noo, dae ye hear. An if ah git wind o you tamperin again wi ma name, ur oney o mine, ah wull hing you oot tae dry!" Ma fist is clenched noo, no faur fae daen hur injury. Ma een ur burnin in ma heid an there is nae soond fae Isa Cameron. The struggle tae haud hur tongue is gein hur trouble, ah kin see that. An the silence pushes ma temper beyoand the bounds.

"An jist so, fur wance, ah kin be furst wi somethin about ma ain affairs," ah snarl it hur. "Ah'll tell ye richt noo, ah'm tae mairry the meenistur. You that's sae foand o fires kin stick that in yer pipe an smoke it!" Isa Cameron stares, her mooth gapes open like a fish oan a slab. Ah luk roon an see thum aw likewies. Wi a snoart, ah turn oan ma heel an mairch back hame. Hauf wey there, Martha Douglas gits a haud o ma airm.

"Och, Ella," she says. "Ah'm fair pleased fur ye." The bubble o anger ah hud roon aboot me bursts. Ma haun goes tae ma mooth an ah stare it hur.

"Whit huv ah done," ah cannae believe it. "Ah wis tae say no!" Martha grins an pats ma airm.

"Then Goad bless Isa Cameron, that's whit ah say." An she goes aff doon the road cairryin hursell fair fu o excitemint. The ithers ur shiftin tae. Ants scartin aff a pile o sugar. Aw the village kens noo. Aw barr wan. Ah set ma shouders square an walk oan intae the hoose.

The lassies ur sittin whaur ah left thum though ah ken fine they've bin it the windae watchin. Aw they'll huv heard wid be the smirl o vices fae the street. Ah'm huvin trouble wi ma braith noo. Kin haurly git oot whit ah huv tae say.

"We'll hae nae mair trouble wi Isa Cameron," ah tell thum. "An ye micht is weel ken, fur ah jist telt them. Ah'm gaun tae mairry Mr Thomson." Ah pit ma coat oan. Gaunae need it noo ah'v nae temper left tae keep me warum. Ah gied oot the wurds like a man gien a punch. Noo ah must haud tae thum. Ah go back oot intae the street. The meenistur will huv his answer.

FULL FLOOD

When we found out new folk had finally moved into the Breckin place, we were all excited. All except our June. She was fifteen. Just. And fifteen, she reckoned, was too old to get excited. Even about the boy.

"In or out of nappies?" She asked.

I groaned. Sometimes she was really annoying. Alec Forrest answered. Rigghall farm is just above the Breckin place so he'd seen them arriving.

"Our age," he said. "Maybe older."

"But not much," Tish and Tosh spoke together. It was a habit they had, being twins. And the names weren't our idea. Tish was really Patricia. And Tosh, well, his folk had seen fit to name him MacIntosh. MacIntosh Gary. As if red hair and freckles weren't enough.

The twins were fourteen. A year older than me. And Alec was the same age as our June. So we all kind of fitted together. What with the Gary farm down in the hollow, and ours this side of the hill, Breckin ridge belonged to us. The Breckin place had no land. It was just a rambling old house. But it sounded like the new boy would fit in fine, just fine.

June slid off the swing and walked down the garden a bit while we waited for her to decide. She turned round with a

sigh.

"He's probably stuck up, spotty and a wimp," she said. "But I suppose we better go take a look."

We all whooped and set off. Alec and June led the way as they usually did. The twins fell in beside me.

"He's not spotty, Beth," Tish hissed. " I seen them driving through the village on their way up here. He looks nice."

"Soft, though," Tosh added while Tish glared at him. "Town folk, I bet. Nice car, though."

They were both right. Ben Drury had black hair, white skin and soft hands. He was sixteen, a head taller than June, and I'd have to say he was good looking. But the closest he'd been to a cow was a pint of milk. He was clever, but he knew nothing about nothing.

He didn't seem surprised though, to see us all sitting on the mound at the back of his new house when he came out to put some rubbish in the bin. Cool as you like, when he spotted us, he came right on over and introduced himself.

There was an awkward pause while we waited for June to speak first. She usually did. When she didn't, Alec had to jump into the space. Alec's kind of thin and wiry, with sandy coloured hair. He went a bit red being put on the spot like that so we all crowded round Ben, trying to cover for June not doing the necessaries.

"Didn't expect a welcoming party," Ben said. "Want to come in and meet the folks?" Alec flushed deeper and hesitated, then he grinned.

"Sure," he said. "We'll give you a hand, if you like."

"Done." Ben shook his hand and we all trooped into the house, even June.

Ben's folk were elderly. If you hadn't known, you'd have guessed they were his grandparents. But they were nice and before long we were all mucking in, shifting boxes to rooms for unpacking later, moving furniture to where Mrs Drury thought she wanted it, and then moving it back again. Finally, when we were all sweating and dust covered, Ben's parents were satisfied.

We shared fruit juice and scones in the kitchen with a lot of banter going on now that the ice was properly broken. Only June was still a bit standoffish, but nobody noticed except me, and maybe Ben. I saw him look towards her a time or two but she wouldn't be drawn into the chatter. It was her decided we should go. She stood up.

"Thanks for your hospitality, Mrs Drury," she said, in her best visiting voice. "Nice to have met you all but we have to be going now. We'll be expected to help with the milking."

She closed my open mouth with one of her special just-you-dare-say-a-word looks and we all took the hint and trooped out. Ben followed, answering Tish's hurried questions about did he have a bike and would he like to come down the Canyon with us the next day. With that settled, we scattered in the different directions of our homes. Ben stopped June and me at the garden gate.

"I could come with you now the work's done," he said. "Meet your folks. And you could show me how to milk a cow."

"We couldn't possibly," June smiled her sweetest smile. "You might get lost on the way back."

Then she turned and swept out of the gate, hurrying over the hill so I had to run to keep up with her.

"Milking?" I gasped. "When did you last help with the milking?"

She glared at me.

"Did you get him, Mr I'm-fair-full-of-myself," she said. "Going to college, he is. Computers, indeed. Needn't think he can come in here and start lording it."

"He was just being nice," I protested. She didn't answer and we went the rest of the way with an unusual silence tripping between us.

Next morning we were whistled out of bed. It was Alec and the twins, all raring to go. And Ben was already with them. June stuck her head out the window and jumped back in again hastily.

"See what they want," she ordered, and rushed over to the mirror to fix her hair.

"Come on," Tosh shouted up. "We've got picnic lunches, so get your gear on, and mind we've not got all day."

We had as it so happened. It was the middle of the school holidays but I was out there in a flash, still tugging the zipper up on my jeans and manhandling my bike at the same time. It took June twice as long as usual to join us.

But we had a good day at the Canyon, an old quarry down in the valley which has great tracks for biking round and a flat floor, dust dry and hard. Ben was good on his machine, knew every trick in the book and spent some time teaching Alec how to do a rear wheel spin on the spot.

Even June was impressed. When she tried it too, and fell off, Ben helped her up. And she didn't shake him off as quick as I thought she might. But she didn't try it again either.

It took another couple of weeks for June to get back to normal. We were down at the Sieve, the pool where the water comes down off the falls. There wasn't much water. There hadn't been any rain for weeks. We had our costumes on but all we'd got was muddy.

Me and Alec were having a race up the two tallest trees beside the water when I spotted June and Ben walking up the slope to the top of the fall. Ben had his arm draped round June's shoulder and she didn't seem to be minding at all.

"See that?" I nodded for Alec to look in their direction. He wasn't much interested, just stopped climbing and skittered back down his tree, breaking twigs as he went. By the time I got down, he was standing at the edge of the water skimming stones over the top of the dwindling pool.

But June was June again, telling us what to do, deciding where we should go. Sometimes she deferred to Ben, him being the newcomer and wanting to get to know the district. But mostly we fell back into our old way of doing things. The only real difference was June and Ben were up front now and Alec hung back with Tosh, leaving me and Tish to trail behind.

The other difference was just a funny feeling I had. Tish said it was the weather, too hot for too long. The sky just sat there like an upturned baking bowl. Maybe that's why Alec's neck looked redder than usual. Maybe that's why, when Tish and me started an arm wrestling contest and June said it was childish, Alec ignored her.

"Come on, Ben," he repeated. "Me and you, huh?" We all knew Alec would win. Ben didn't do farm work. But, in the middle of it, with them stretched full length on the burnt grass, knuckles white, teeth clenched and staring into each other's eyes, the fun suddenly went out of it. June got on her bike and went home.

Then, like most summers when it stays dry too much, the rain didn't want to go off once it got started. We were stuck inside for three days and, being farming folk, got pretty wound up about it. Our folks went from worrying about lack of water for the crops, to watching a lot of the grain being battered into the ground. When it finally dried up on the fourth day, we were glad to get out and away from the tension in the house.

Because there'd been water and the sun was warm again, we automatically headed for the Sieve. But whenever we got there we knew there'd be no swimming. The burn was in spate, the falls spilled an avalanche of water into the basin and we could see the swirls on the pool from the rock configuration underneath, and from which the Sieve got its name.

Ben stripped off to his trunks.

"We can't swim in there," Alec said.

"Why not?"

"The currents," Alec explained. "Suck you under."

Ben turned and looked at June. She only shrugged. He looked back at Alec. I felt like we hadn't got away from the tension back home after all. We'd brought it with us.

"You scared?" Ben smiled one of his slow smiles at Alec who shook his head just as slowly and didn't take his eyes off Ben's face.

"Nope," he said. "Just being sensible." Ben laughed out loud then.

"I'll race you across," he said. Everything seemed to go into slow motion then. I saw Alec look towards June, waiting, like the rest of us, for her to tell Ben it wasn't on. For her to stop it. June looked right back and said nothing. Alec went very red.

He had his clothes hauled off before any of the rest of us could speak. They both hit the water together, and disappeared. It seemed an age before they surfaced, side by side, both swimming hard. Whatever was in the air had gotten to us all. Tish and Tosh were shouting them both on, turn about.

"Go on, Ben. Go on, Alec."

I looked at June, standing back against the trees as if frozen to the spot. The look in her eyes scared me.

"Come back," I screamed at the two swimmers. "Come back."

It was already too late. Ben's head vanished under the water. And I could see the tell-tale swirl of foam close to where he went down.

"Alec!" I screamed. He turned, saw the empty space behind him, and vanished under the black surface too. I looked wildly at June. She was the strongest swimmer of us all. And she stood rooted where she was. I flung my dress off, yelled at Tish and Tosh to get branches down, and dived.

When I surfaced I saw Alec's head pop up again. I wanted to shout to him to leave Ben and get himself out but had to save my breath. The current pulled on my legs, slowing me down. By the time I got near, Alec had gone again. I trod water. He popped up just in front of me.

"Help me," he gasped, and I could see he had a grip of something. I felt down his arm to Ben's hair. Together we hauled him high enough to grip an arm each and somehow, somehow we managed to reach back for the branch the twins had pushed towards us. Worn out and swallowing water, we kicked and were pulled back to the edge.

The twins got Ben out, turned him over and started pumping the water out of him. Coughing and spluttering, Alec and I dragged ourselves onto the rock. By the time we got the river shook out of us, we could hear Ben being sick at our backs. We hung onto each other, laughing and crying at the same time.

When I finally looked about for June, she had gone. There was nothing to do then but get Ben, shaking and shivering, home to be dried out before we could all do the same.

At the yew tree, where Alec always left us for his farm, I asked him why he'd gone in. His eyes looked haunted, and his face was paler than I'd ever seen it.

"Ask June," he said, and he walked away over the fields.

WIDDERSHINS

An wha's tae say ah wis wrang? Ah seen thum thegither. Ah seen thum go on the pub, an it Wednesday. An ah'd seen thum afore. Doon the Steckie whin awbody else wis workin. He wis haudin hur fit. Haudin it up an dryin it oan a white hankie. An hur sittin leanin back oan the bank wi hur leg, shinin wet fae the watter, streeched up tae him an hur fit airched in his haun. Ah seen thum.

Ah clattert the poats an pans the nicht, steerin masell up, ye'll ken. There wis nuthin else fur it bit tae tell him. He wis huvin a bit read o the paper, wi his bitts aff an the damp stull steamin oot his soaks it the fire. Ah went ben an riddled the coals.

"Mither," he says. "Ye'll be gaun doon through that grate the noo if ye dinnae caw caunny. Whit's up wi ye?"

"Me," says I. "Whit wid be up wi me?" He shiftit in his sate an the paper fell ower oan itsell.

"Weel, ye'll be seein daylicht through they pats the morra," he says. "Fur ah doot ye've left a bottum in thum. Ye're nivir this het up ower a coupla pun o berries?"

"Naw, ah'm no. Though ah pued thum masell, mind. Bit ah'll hae burnt worse than some wild rasps in ma time, nae doot." Ah draw braith. "It's your Ellen hus goat ma heid burlin."

There, it wis oot an his chin comes furrit, jist like his faither's yaised tae, wi his broos doon.

"Whey's that?" He says, thin like. So ah tell him. Wednesday, whin she disnae work Wednesday. An doon the Steckie this efternin, paddlin like bairns an dryin each ither. Ye kin tell a loat fae a touch. He flung the paper oan the flair an goat up.

"Ye're no gaun doon there," says I. He's pittin his bitts oan, no even his guid shune. An ah ken whit he sees. Donald's flat abin the pub, an the twa o thum up there. Alane. Thegither. The waw shakes wi the door shuttin it his back. It's a wunner the gless is stull hale.

An it's no jist ma heid that's burlin. Ma stomach's cawin roon, fair hoat an jumpin. Goad gie him the patience tae fund oot whit he needs tae fund oot, an lit him keep his temper. Ah kent she wid nivir be guid fur him. There's no a man passes hur withoot lukin. See it in the wey she walks. Like a cat, aw smooth an flowin. Queenin it. Bit she'll no ful a Cameron laddie. Ah'll see tae that.

The waitin kills me, an ah huv tae wait. The daurk's creepin in an feet comin hame rattle the quate. Bit nivir a fit oan oor path, nivir a scrape oan the step. Ah staun it till ah kin staun it nae mair, pit a scarf ower ma heid an go oot intae the street. It seems a lang wey doon the road tae the pub, an awbody's in thur beds, an it the only licht that's stull shinin.

The door openin cuts a bricht wedge oot the daurk an they're there, the twa o thum, no ten fit awa an Sandy's airm roon hur shouders. She flicks hur hair tae wan side an luks up it him.

"Ye've bin fetcht," she says an goes tae step sideweys awa fae him. He disnae lit go, draws hur back wi his airm stull roon hur shouder. His een ur orange in the street licht. The fire in ma stomach turns tae chips o ice.

"Ah'm steyin it Ellen's," he says. "Ah'll git ma stuff the morra."

"Ye micht wait till ye're wed," ah say. "Fowk'll talk." He

smirks, an it isnae a laugh. His vice is cauld, cauld.

"They wur checkin the stock," he says. "There's talk fur ye." They baith turn awa.

Bit there's stull the Steckie. Ah kin see that curve o broon leg yit, sparklin wet, an fingurs strokin the airch o hur fit.

"Ye cannae say ah'm wrang," ah shout.

He disnae answer. She luks it me, yin eebroo up, mockin. They walk oan ower the road an she's hirplin. Favourin hur richt fit. An ah'm bate, peened wi fury. There's a strip o white bandage showin, bund roon, inside hur shune.

YON CAT

The kitten was black as soot. A black pom-pom with tiger claws. The four of us stared. Round, china blue eyes stared back.

"He's mine." Peggy made a grab. Tam shoved her aside.

"Naw, he's no. He's a Tom cat."

"That," Liz turned on him, "disnae make him yours, Tam." Me, ever the peacemaker.

"Look, ah'm the auldest -" All three burled round, aggrieved and voluble. The kitten blinked, unhinged its jaw in a pink-throated yawn, scratched behind its ear and fell over, completely indifferent. Our Mam, who'd produced this cause of dissension from the mysterious depths of her shopping basket, ended our squabble with three words.

"Ah'll droon it."

So the kitten was never allocated. Or named either. It was referred to as *Yon Cat*. And that was Granda's doing. From his armchair by the fire he watched silently as we all mooned admiringly over the bundle of nails, spit and fluff that rolled on the carpet at his feet. Then he took his pipe out of his mouth. It was a move that meant he was going to speak. A move that always met with silence.

"Yon cat'll be nowt but trouble," he said in his slow,

deliberate way. "Oney fool kin keep a cat an fund oot. If they've a mind." He stuck the pipe back in his mouth, teeth clamped on the step. It was seldom lit though a lot of Granda's time was spent in the lighting of it. Granda hated cats. Useless beasts, he thought them.

Our ball of fluff grew bigger, blacker, fluffier. There was no sleek, smooth coat for yon cat. He became the biggest tom cat in the village and his fluffed out coat advertised the fact. As he grew our interest in him diminished, as did his interest in us. Things flourished in the fields and houses round about that challenged him more than our childish games - birds, mice, lady cats. He was seldom home. And then only to sleep.

Strange thing was he never learned Granda hated cats. It was Granda's lap he curled up in when he deigned to visit. Granda's knee he sought after a night's courtship. And when Granda wasn't available he'd settle in a huff on top of the coal pail. Many a time he was nearly thrown on the fire by mistake.

Our attention, meanwhile, turned to other things. Bill Johnstone, next door, began building a large shed on his green though he'd a shed already and what would he be wanting with two. He wouldn't tell. We hung on the paling and watched, plying him with all the questions we dared. When we tired of this, we hung upside down from the top metal bar to see how it looked from that angle.

Granda appeared for a wander round the green, went down to the vegetable patch for a bit look at the brussel sprouts, and wandered back again. He stopped behind us, looked over at the rising wood of the shed and took the pipe out of his mouth. We waited, hung like bats on the fence. Granda would get to the bottom of this.

"Fine day," he said. Bill Johnstone nodded and drove in another nail. Granda put the pipe back in his mouth. We all collapsed in humps on the grass.

The disappointment didn't last long. The shed, with its ledge and sliding shutters, was filled one day with a noise like water bubbling down a drain. Pigeons. We rushed back in to tell. Granda drew the pipe out of his mouth.

"Yon pigeons'll be nowt but trouble," he said. "Oney fool kin keep pigeons an fund oot. If they've a mind." Granda hated pigeons.

We soon found out why. His best shirt came in off the rope with splatter all over it. We were shushed and sent indoors whenever Bill had them out racing. The cat, which Bill had never minded before, became the enemy and often dived for cover of the open back door with Bill and the besom behind him. Granda raised his newspaper so his whole face was hidden every time Bill was heard out on the back green, rattling his tin of pigeon peas and calling to his birds.

The excitement of the pigeons lasted till the end of the year when Eric Sneddon provided us with another novelty. A hutch like a rabbit hutch appeared outside his back door. We climbed on the opposite paling this time and peered across Sam Anderson's coal bunker to survey this devlopment. A slim white shape darted past the wire netting front. It was no rabbit. Nor a guinea pig either.

"It's a ferret," Eric shouted back. No secrets with him.

Behind us, Bill Johnstone was out cushying his cushy doos. Eric's shout stopped him in his tracks.

"A ferret, did ye say?" He yelled. "Is that a ferret?" He sounded loud, but then he'd to carry over two back greens for Eric to hear him. We all turned round to look. He looked loud. A red flush made his heavy jowls hang lower on his shirt than normal. Eric let him know it was that exactly. A ferret. You could tell he was proud the way he said it.

"Ah'll be havin rabbit pie reg'lar," he boasted. Bill's jowls quivered.

"Ah hope it's jist *Rabbit* pie ye mean tae huv," he roared.

Sam Anderson appeared at his door, axe in one hand, shovel

in the other to make it look like the want of coal had brought him out and not the din. He leaned over to peer into the hutch, pronounced the ferret a bonny specimen then sauntered casual over to where we perched by his bunker. His hand rose to lift the lid and halted in mid-air. In front of our eight eyes we saw, for the first time though we'd been peering over it a good half hour, that the lid of the bunker was gone.

Hand poised, Sam's head spun round to stare at Eric, or more especially at Eric's ferret hutch, with a new perspective. He remarked what a fine bit of wood it was made from.

"Reminds me o ma bunker," he went on. "Specially the lid!"

Eric caught on and protested.

"Never mind your bunker," Bill roared at our backs again. "What aboot ma pigeons? That hutch better be strong."

Sam swung round to face Bill.

"It'll be strong right enough," he shouted back. "Isn't it made wi ma bunker lid!" We were having trouble staying on the fence and keeping twirling our heads round to the action. Eric was next.

"It cannae git oot," he assured Bill. "Ah put a padlock oan it."

Sam swung the axe up, wrong way round.

"Some o us should be pittin padlocks oan oor bunkers," he growled. "Mibbe that wey we'd keep oor lids!" The blunt end of the axe crashed down on the huge lumps of coal breaking them into fire size. We slunk away indoors.

Granda sat in his chair, idly trying to light his pipe. Though we knew fine well he'd heard every word we crowded round and repeated what had gone on. Three matches later, when he was sure it was lit, he took the pipe from his teeth.

"Yon ferret'll be nowt but trouble," he said. "Oney fool kin keep a ferret an fund oot. If they've a mind." Granda hated ferrets. Dirty smelling things he said they were. Not to be trusted.

We soon found out they were not a lot of fun either. Not after it had the top off Tam's pinkie and he had to be rushed for tetanus shots. This meant our doctor decided we'd just as well all have injections, to be on the safe side. None of us were ever fond of ferrets after that. And the ferret never encouraged our friendship. It didn't eat carrots or dandelions. Just the top of Tam's pinkie. We paid homage from the paling from then on.

The homage it earned. A good supply of rabbits came Eric's way that winter. Each week-end he'd set off for the woods with nets, stakes and mallet in a bag over his shoulder while the ferret danced, trapped in a thick canvas flour sack that swung from Eric's other hand.

When spring came and the snow melted from the top of Sam's lidless bunker, the pigeons came into their own again. Bill had them out as often as the weather was promising while he waited their homecoming, clock in one hand, the infernal pigeon peas in the other.

Then one day it happened. A blood freezing screech rose into the air from outside and through the open kitchen door came yon cat. Its fur stood out stark from its body. Tail starched erect and stiff-legged, it shot past our Mam into the livingroom. That terrible sound from its throat screamed the full circle it stoated round the room. Then it couped over, stiff as a board and stone dead.

We all stared. Tam, the brave as ever Tam, prodded it gently with the toe of his boot. It was dead all right, a strange twisted grin frozen on its face. Granda took his pipe out of his mouth.

"Pisened," he said. "Plain as day."

We buried the cat at the bottom of the garden, pulling up some of the stripped sprout stalks to make space for the cemetery. Granda dug the hole. We all stood solemn round about. It was our first family burial and a moving occasion. Liz read a bit from the Bible. Peggy cried. I had made a cross from two white sticks stripped of bark. Yon Cat, Tam had burned in the bare wood. Together we tapped it into the freshly turned earth.

Granda was quiet for some weeks after that. Knowing how he'd hated yon cat we all made a point of not referring to its sudden demise in his hearing. But before long he took to going out for his walks again and was often out on the back green enjoying what fresher air could sneak past the funnel of smoke from his pipe.

We heard Bill getting onto him one day about how well his pigeons were doing and how they were in line for the big cup.

"Just wan mair race," he crowed. "That's aw ah need."

Granda thought winning the trophy would be a fine thing.

"Be a rare big shiny cup," he said. "Look richt grand oan yer sideboard, wull it?"

"It wull that." Bill's jowls wobbled in happy agreement.

Granda was quiet again that night. Ready for his usual evening walk, we saw him fold a small, thick canvas flour sack into his greatcoat pocket. He was still quiet.

Early next morning the quiet was broken. A screech, in ghostly imitation of yon cat's last sound, issued from the gardens. Only this screech settled into a low moaning wail. We were all out of doors in our nightwear, hopping on the dew wet grass.

Bill, blood streaked and whimpering, sat on the step of his pigeon loft. In his thick hands he nursed the limp, torn body of one of his precious pigeons. Behind him the door of the loft swung open. There was mayhem inside. Feathers drifted and floated round. Spatters of pigeon blood were everywhere. The sound of bubbling water had ceased.

We all knew it was the ferret. A glance at the hutch showed it empty, the wire mesh front tugged down at the corner. The work of a beast created to kill and deprived by the breeding season. None of us had heart enough to speak.

After a while Granda came out of the house. Bill lifted grieving eyes and found his voice. He damned the ferret and poor simple Eric for all eternity. He moaned for the lost hopes of the prized cup, mourned his savaged pigeons, his pets, his treasures. He went on at length.

Granda tapped out his pipe on the fence and refilled it from the pouch he kept in his back pocket.

"Dae ye mind wee Bluey," Bill went on. "Fastest wee burd ever was. An dae ye mind Pinkie? Wan cushy-cushy an she was in."

Granda stuck the filled pipe back in his mouth.

"An dae ye mind Redeye -," Bill began another.

The pipe was jerked out Granda's mouth.

"An dae you mind yon cat?" He snapped. Bill's head came up. "Whit cat?"

"Yon cat," Granda said. "Yon cat whit came screamin in an couped ower stiff as a board an stane deid. Whit's buried doon there." The pipe waved. "Yon cat!"

Bill remembered. Remembered he'd seen it happen.

"Aye," he said. "We've baith cause fur grievance wi oor neeburs."

Granda's pipe stopped waving in the air.

"Ah was at ma pigeons that day when Sam came oot fur the coal," Bill went on. "But isn't it still that Eric's fault fur havin the lid aff the bunker."

The fire died in Granda's eyes as Bill talked. The cat had been sleeping on the coal in the sun. Sam never even saw it, black as it was. Just swung the blunt end of the axe down to break up the coal.

"He must've near deid whin the cat whirled up at him, screechin an screamin an stoated aff intae the hoose." Bill shook his head. "Must've been aw the wey inside afore it noticed Sam hud killed it."

Granda stared at Bill for a long time. Then he stuck the pipe back in his mouth. Bill continued the interrupted litany for his pigeons. Granda fetched the key for the hut and took out a spade.

We all followed him to the vegetable patch at the bottom of the garden. We all looked on as he dug up the overgrown grave. Yon cat had changed some, but not much. Its face was still twisted in that strange grin. But time had revealed the reason for it. A great hole gaped in the top of yon cat's skull.

We stared from the cat to Granda. Silent, he filled the earth back over the cat. Silent, he put the spade back in the hut. And, silent, he went indoors to sit in his chair.

TALK WITHOOT WURDS

Tyin the rope, ah'm tryin haurd tae mind whin ah last tied a knoat in oneything. Ma mither hud a sayin aboot ropes, aboot tyin a knoat in it. Bit ah cannae jist mind whit it wis. Oneywey, this is a different kinna knoat an that wis a lang time ago. Must be thurty year since ma mither deid. Sometimes, sometimes ah kin believe time husnae passed. Sometimes ah kin hear hur vice, sayin somethin perfectly oardinry, in a perfectly oardinry tone ae vice. Is if time husnae moved oan at aw. Is if she's no deid an burrit these thurty years bit stull sittin in hur chair, in the coarnur, bi the fire.

Huvnae heard hur vice fur a while. Huvnae heard oney vice fur a lang while. Mind, ah wis in the paper shoap this moarnin, is usual. An Meg McKay spoke tae me. She ayewis dis. Bit ah cannae mind whit wis said. Nur whit ah answert. If ah answert. Which ah probably did. Must hae bin aboot the weathur. Din't fowk talk aboot the weathur ninety purcent ae the time. Ah read that somewhaur wance. Ninety purcent. That's an awfy loat ae talk. Bit then, there's an awfy loat ae weathur tae talk aboot.

The last vice ah mind hearin wis auld Pete McFarlin's. Pete's crumlin, whitewaasht coattage wis last oan ma route. He deid last year, in the spring. Spring, he yaised tae say it gleddened an auld man's hert. Mibbe it wis the quickenin that made his gie oot. Wha kid tell. Ah try the knoat. It's no bad at aw. No bad at aw. Aye, Pete's wis the last vice ah really heard. That wis twa year ago. Whin ah stull delivert the poast. Oan the same day ah retired.

"Aye, things chainge," he sayd. "Bit they dinnae chainge much." He wis wrang, is usual, gein he hud a habit ae makin sweepin statemints. Things chainge a loat. That young couple wha bocht his hoose stoapt the crumlin, It luks dustit an poalished noo, wi a gairidge tae hoose thur shiny rid forin caur an a paved patio whaur Pete's gairden hud wance hoastit every kinna weed in the district. Life dis chainge. S'only burth an daith stey the same. Naebody hus yit figured oot a new wey fur fowk tae git intae the wurld, fur aw thur tryin. An naebody kens oney ither wey ootae it, eithur.

It wis sunny thon day. Ma last day. Pete met me it the door in his shurt sleeves. He liked tae come tae the door.

"Saves me the bother've bendin," he sayd. "Micht no straughten up if ah bend whin ma back's no expectin it." Ah gied him his lettur. Fae his son in Canada, it wis. Regulur, every month. Mibbe Rab Coannell hudnae waitit fur Pete tae git tae the door an open it. Mibbe Pete hudnae bin able tae straughten up. Ah feenish aff the knoat. Ma hauns urnae is guid is they micht be. Stiff. Bit the knoat's fine.

Ah feenished up oan the poast that same day. Feenished ma roond, hung ma seck up oan the hook, haundit ower ma unifurm an retired. Efter twinty five year. Twinty five year o early rises, up afore the burds, alang the road tae collect the mail bag fae the early bus an intae the poast oaffice in the shoap tae soart it oot fur delivry. Daurk moarnins wur best. Feelin furst up, hearin the soond ae ma ain feet comin back, the village creepin ootae sleep roon aboot me. There wis a rogue burd in the village then. It wid sing sometimes whin ah walked alang Rose street tae the shoap. A blackburd that shouldae bin asleep. Mibbe it wis dreamin. Singin is it dreamt o sun an summur, driftin speedurs an greedy young.

No that ah taen time tae wunner. Naw. Ye jist accept. Whit is, is. A burd singin in the daurk. An auld man wha cannae bend. Mail waitin fur delivry. Bessie Joanson writin tae oor M.P. again, a summuns fur the Barbours, burthday fur the Cameron laddie. Aw the business ae a normul, busy, livin cummunity. That's whey ah cannae write a lettur. There's nuthin tae say. An the mail ayewis sayd mair tae me than fowk. Fowk talk tae me the wey they talk tae the doctur.

"Is there a lettur fur me, Nancy?" Hauf wey up the street an ah'd tae go in ma bag an search it oot. Ur, "By, it's blawin a blizzurd. Ye'll be gled tae be done the day." True, an no true. Ah aye felt heroic in the snaw. Brave in the battle fur progress. An sometimes, "A parsul. Fur us?" Aye wished ah'd bin blessed wi the black sense ae humur that wid lit me grab it back again sayin, "Naw, it cannae be. Must hae your name oan it bi mistake."

Ah wis nivir ower foand ae parsuls. Awkwurd an heavy, they meant a wait it the door fur somebody tae open it. Naw. Fowk like parsuls bit there wis nae joay in thum fur me. Parsuls micht be oneything. No like letturs. Money in this wan, a daith in that. Legul letturs, new bairns, wurd aboot freens ur faimly, business, wurk ur worry. Like a lang, deep conversation. Bettur, even. Talk withoot wurds.

Tether, that wis the wurd ma mither yaised. Tether, no rope. Whin ye reach the end ae yer tether, tie a knoat in it. That wis it. Ur wis it? Disnae seem richt, somehoo. The wurds jist hing there, no quite feenished. The chair shoogles an ah've tae steady masell. Widnae waant tae mak a mess ae this.

Even the extra wurk o the electric bills didnae bothur me. Tam Paine in a bad mood. He's three dochturs an lichts that stey oan tae efter midnicht. Blaws a fuse aboot every bill bit nivir dis oneything tae cut doon. He jist resents peyin fur somethin that seems is effurtlis and naturul tae come by is rain must seem tae gress. Bit auld Pete wis stull wrang. Tom Pain's lassies'll grow up an leave. His bills'll shrivul. He'll wunner whit tae blaw his stack aboot then. Wunner whey he waistit sae much time bein angry whin aw he hud tae dae wis flick a switch the ither wey.

The rope's rough in ma hauns, heavy oan ma coallur bone. Things chainge aw richt. Ah slide the knoat ticht. An mind noo whit ma mither yaised tae say. "Tie a knoat in it an hing oan." Mibbe ah'll be smilin. It's aw ye kin dae. An it means nuthin. Nuthin at aw. Time ... tae kick the chair awa.

RHYTHM OF THE BLUES

The voice at the other end of the phone sounded warm, friendly and inviting.

"Mr Spalding? If I could take up a few minutes of your time -" The burr in her voice brought him up short. Jenna's ghost. The voice lilted on, cutting him with a knife she didn't know she possessed. He rubbed his fingers in the fortnight's growth on his jaw, searching in the stubble for anything that didn't belong there. He could just picture her, at the other end of the phone, sitting on her padded telephone seat in her navy blue serge skirt and pale blue twinset. With her neat list of bought and paid for names. But wearing Jenna's face. Talking with Jenna's voice.

"Sod off."

"Pardon?"

"I don't want no double glazing. Ain't got no bleeding window. This here's a bleeding cell, sweetheart. Get off the sodding phone."

The silence lasted all the way from his ear to the receiver rest.

Now he put his two hands down on either side of the silent instrument and rocked forwards over it, nursing the ache that was hard and heavy just under his ribs. When it didn't ease he sat down heavily on the bed behind him and reached for the glass and bottle he'd left on the cabinet beside the top of the bed.

The glass was tacky in his hand but he tipped whisky into it, sat the bottle down on the frayed carpet by his feet and rolled the glass back and forth along the grimy fingers of his two hands. With a sharp jerk, he tossed a swallow of whisky back into his throat.

"God damn you, Jenna."

On either side of the telephone his hands had left two perfect prints in the dust.

He had lied about the window. It was beside the cooker in the part of the room that served as a kitchen. True it had bars, on the outside for it was four floors up. A long narrow window hung with grimy blue gingham curtains. Even in the daytime it didn't let in much light. Now it was dark outside. Dark inside too, for the single light bulb had given up the ghost some time before and never been replaced. The light that danced on the wall behind the bed was the reflected filtered colours from the neon sign of the Jazz club across the street. The sound in the room was the muted rhythm of the blues, as if a radio played half-loud in the room next door.

It was in the Jazz club he'd met Jenna. That was where he'd hung about nights, where he met with John D and Sloopy to talk form and swop tips. She'd come in with Myra, Sloopy's woman. They'd adopted each other in the public toilets of the cafe Myra waitressed in daytimes. Another soft voiced runaway, new to the Smoke. The city would chew her up.

He could read her easy then. It was in her eyes when she looked at him till she dropped her lashes to cover it, her fingers suddenly distracted by a scar in the arm of her chair that must be picked at. So he'd waited until she was in tune with the company and relaxed, then he'd leaned over the table.

"Got a bunk yet, have you?" She shook her head, the curtain of dark hair down her back drifted an echo of the move. "You have now. If you want it."

To make sure he took her up to dance. She'd cottoned on his nickname.

"Kipper?"

"Account of me hair."

Other couples, draped over each other, shuffled about the small floor. On the platform beside them, trapped in the white shaft of light and with her eyes half closed, Stella sang the blues.

"Emotion," Jenna said. He watched blue smoke curl round Stella's black chins and drift past the white rims of her upturned closed eyes to collect in the cloud under the ceiling lights.

"Smoke," he told her.

He tossed back the mouthful of whisky still in the glass and poured another. Then he stood up and walked over to the window. At the end of the first week she hung the blue gingham curtains.

"Can't think why you bother," he'd told her. Still couldn't. There were only the pigeons to know.

Down across the street people came and went through the club doors. He watched them, peering against the trickling colours of the sign to make out the shapes. He'd watched a lot from the window when she'd first gone, knowing she had to come back. Once he'd seen her, the long black hair, the easy walk. He banged out the door, down the flights of stairs and across the street. In the club he couldn't see her. Sloopy and John D sat in their regular space. He slammed his fist on the table.

"Jenna," he said. "She came in here." Sloopy shook his head.

"She ain't here, man. Gone, ain't she." He stumbled away from them, shaking John D's hand from his arm. He could drink in his room. She'd gone all right. She'd taken his luck with her.

He should phone the Fatman. His fingers searched in the pockets of his jeans, teasing out two crumpled notes, one of them a tenner. He could make a call. There was a bitch due to run at the Stadium he'd heard good things about. Or that filly at Newmarket tomorrow, right on form she was and good odds too. First time out this season, she'd been saved for this one. Only he couldn't make the call. He was all out of credit with the Fatman. It would have to be cash on the line and that not till tomorrow. He hadn't made a call in over a week.

The bottle of whisky stood by the phone. He squinted over at it from the window. Even in the dim changing light he could see the liquid glow inside the glass. It was half full. A grin twisted his mouth. He stuck the crumpled notes back in his pocket, the itch to make the phone call gone. The bottle was half empty.

He walked over to re-fill his glass and his arm caught the handle of a pot that sat on the cooker, brought it clattering to the floor. Stooping he picked it up. A few shrivelled beans stuck in the bottom, each circled with white where the sauce had dried and shrunk away from them. He dropped the pot in the sink, chipping another dent in the pock-marked enamel.

He tried to remember what it was like when Jenna was there. Times they'd bought up new clothes and gone up town to some posh place for food. And once there'd been enough to go crazy with. He'd honked on the horn of the white two-seater and they'd driven out of town with the top rolled down in the rain to a place he'd visited as a boy. They'd swum naked in a pool under a canopy of dripping leaves and made love in the long grass which was wet and squeaked under their backsides. Some things were easy to remember.

He swallowed more of the whisky and yanked open the drawer by the sink looking for a smoke. The buff coloured cards lay scattered inside it. Calling cards of things come and gone, most of them with the pawnbrokers stamp long overdue. A picture of Jenna floated in his head. She was drawing a smiling face on a dusty TV screen.

"Hey you," she said. "You only come here to visit."

He found the cigarettes, a few left in the pack, tried to light one from the gas before he remembered he hadn't fed the meter in a couple of days. Last time he'd thought about the pawnbroker was because of the baby. Well. it wasn't a real baby. Not the pink, squalling, live kind. But the problem kind. It had filled him with panic. Someplace in his throat the panic turned to rage.

"You crazy or something," he screamed at her. "Where're you going to put a baby in here, for Christsake." He saw from her eyes he was taking the fence too hard. " Sod it, Jenna, we're just starting up." She banged open the drawer, grabbed a handful of the buff coloured cards and flung them in his face.

"Starting up?" She'd shouted. "Starting down, you mean."

That had cost his some fast thinking and some fancy work with the Fatman on the telephone. But a week later she'd had it done. The problem sucked out of her and spilled down the drain.

He found a book of matches from the club under the edge of the bed and sat down to enjoy the smoke. The quartet were playing Busted, Greenback's rasping voice toned down by distance and the walls. He looked over at the phone. That bill he always paid. She would call soon now.

She'd called him often after the cousin arrived. John D's cousin, up- from-the-country typical. Tall and clean, he wore a shirt and tie. The ties varied, the shirts stayed the same, clean and pristine white. He was a surprise to them all, especially John D. One more chair was drawn to their table, to be temporary this time. The cousin was no gambler. That was clear from the off. Conversation staggered around and then stopped. The cousin took Jenna up on the floor. Kipper watched the two of them, stiff and strange. The white shirt shone like a beacon in the dark.

"Sorry about the Kid," John D had said. It was Kipper named him Milky Bar. A week later Jenna called, first time he'd heard her voice over the phone. She'd been roped in. Unofficial guide for the tourist season, company for the cousin. He sympathised and went back to marking off the form sheets. Days he sprawled on the bed with his racing guides, pencilling possibles on the newsprint, never far from the telephone. Jenna was always about. Now she called in.

He ground out the cigarette stub and filled his glass again. The bottom of the bottle rose above the rim of the glass. It was the cousin's last week before he noticed. He watched them dance that night. Their bodies fitted together, like a hand in a glove.

"How long's he stopping?" He asked John D.

"Other week."

Seven days later he knew Jenna was going too. Nothing of her lay about the room. She was backed against the sink, her eyes wary as he looked about. He said it for her.

"You're going," he snorted. "With the Milky Bar kid." She nodded. "Nine to five. Grass and cows and hoovers and kids. Who needs it, Jenna?"

"I do, Kipper. I do."

He turned away from her and tried to shut out the sound of the door as it closed behind her. But he knew she'd be back. She'd call some day. When she tired of playing the lily white queen in her hygienic kitchen with her apple cheeked dolls, she'd call. So long as he kept the phone.

He hunched back, leaned on one elbow on the bed and stared at the phone. So long as he kept the phone. He drew back his leg, aimed with the heel of his bare foot and kicked the phone from the table. It shattered with an indignant ping, hiccupped and lay still, the receiver dead on the worn carpet. He squinted at the half inch of scotch glinting in the bottle. From the club he could hear the drum roll that meant Stella had stepped into her spot, trapped in the glare of blue-smoked light.

He lay back on the grubby pillow, raised the bottle to his lips and drunk the dregs. His eyes felt gritty behind his closed lids, dry and sore. Jenna - he could hardly remember who Jenna was. The empty bottle hit the floor with a dull thud as the low sad tones of a female singer fell on the darkened room.

Taranis Fiction

Tales From The Coast
ISBN 1 873899 00 9   £4.99

"It's handsomely produced, with bizarre illustration to suit the off-beat fiction. I like it immensely for its bizarre fun, its unparochial unpredictability, its constant surprises.

   This is a collection which works far better than most... It has a kind of unity, it's always entertaining, and often highly poetic and suggestive. I look forward to regular samples, and salute the magazine."

Douglas Gifford in Books in Scotland

The Gringo Trees by J. William Doswell
ISBN 1 873899 05 X   £4.99

"No review could or should stand in for reading this book. The sheer economy of its prose allows it to develop at a very fast pace and yet leaves the impression of being a much longer book... All in all, **The Gringo Trees** makes a superb debut on the British publishing scene."

David Ross in Northwards

When God Blinked and Other Stories by J. William Doswell
ISBN 1 873899 40 8   £3.99

J. William Doswell is an American who lives in Virginia in the southern part of the United States. A one-time member of the CIA, he has also been a marine, a journalist, a newspaper publisher, and a political lobbyist.

Masel by Mark Smith
ISBN 1 873899 35 1   £5.99

"An energetic, funny, sometimes wise first novel."

The Scotsman

"Deserving of the Glasgow Kiss"

The Herald

Taranis Poetry

The Mating of Dinosaurs by Bill Oliphant
ISBN 1 873899 30 0   £5.99

"...a most accomplished, quirky poet refreshingly unbeholden to any current fashions."

Mario Relich in Lines Review

Ergonomic Work Stations and Spinning Teacans
by Brian Whittingham
ISBN 1 873899 25 4   £4.99

"...includes the poems in his pamphlet Industrial Deafness which I liked very much when it appeared two years ago. In this new, more substantial collection, he shows he is here to stay. He is not afraid to experiment with language. As I have said before, he has the tang of Tom Leonard's Glasgow."

Robin Bell in Books in Scotland

Painting Shadows on the Tilting Horizon by Emil Rado
ISBN 1 873899 45 9   £3.99

"His poetry is not complex... it is pictorial, invigorated with familiarity with crags and rushing streams of Scotland. And yet the writing is intimate, meditative, gentle. The desolations of early childhood have not shrouded his natural enthusiasms and perceptions..."

Charles Kohler in The Friend

The Elementary Particles by Gerry Loose
ISBN 1 873899 60 2   £5.99   Images by Kate Sweeney McGee

The last book from Gerry Loose to appear was Knockariddera (Galdragon Press, 1991). Here is what one critic said:
"The poet has the eye for the place that comes from long working there, long staring at the sky, long battles with the elements. His thoughts, the

poems, fit the place as water will fill a tyre mark or a hoof print and it is wonderful to read this unfolding year and be reminded of things we should not forget."

Taranis Ideas

The Necessary Goat and Other Essays on Formative Thinking
by Alison Prince
ISBN 1 873899 10 6   £6.95

In our formative years we are channelled by our social environment, education and training towards narrow modes of thinking. **The Necessary Goat and Other Essays on Formative Thinking** shows how this imposed mindset results in the blocking of a creative mental function which can have distressing effects.

This stimulating book identifies the importance of art in its most profound sense and the intrinsic role of creativity in the process of living.